Mrs. J. H. Riddel

The Earl's promise

A Novel. Vol. 3

Mrs. J. H. Riddell

The Earl's promise
A Novel. Vol. 3

ISBN/EAN: 9783337046491

Printed in Europe, USA, Canada, Australia, Japan

Cover: Foto ©Andreas Hilbeck / pixelio.de

More available books at **www.hansebooks.com**

THE EARL'S PROMISE.

THE EARL'S PROMISE.

A Novel.

BY

MRS. RIDDELL,

AUTHOR OF

" GEORGE GEITH," " TOO MUCH ALONE," " HOME, SWEET HOME,"
ETC.

IN THREE VOLUMES.

VOL. III.

LONDON:

TINSLEY BROTHERS, 8 CATHERINE STREET, STRAND.

1873.

PRINTED BY TAYLOR AND CO.,
LITTLE QUEEN STREET, LINCOLN'S INN FIELDS.

CONTENTS

OF

THE THIRD VOLUME.

THE EARL'S PROMISE.

CHAPTER I.

LEFT ALL ALONE.

BETWEEN them, Drs. Murney and Connelley devised some plan of treatment designed to comfort Dr. Girvan, to provide the inmates of Bayview with an ideal occupation, and to impress Grace with the conviction that nothing which could be done to save her father was being left undone.

True to his determination, Dr. Girvan, spite of all entreaties to the contrary, broke the news of Mr. Moffat's danger to his daughter, accusing himself, at the same time, with having been the cause of that danger.

"Ye trusted me," he said, in that homely

Irish accent which is never so sweet as when the speaker is in trouble and breathes a pathetic tone with every word,—" Ye trusted me, and this is how I've recompensed ye ; and all because of my own hatred—God forgive me !—and my own conceit. Had it been Dr. Murney or Connelley that said I was wrong, I'd have listened to either of them ; but as it is, my heart is breaking to think about you and him."

Into the old, honest face, puckered with emotion, into the eyes that had looked at her with a kindly light in them so often, Grace gazed for a minute. She was not so besotted with her own grief that she failed to see the bitterer grief of another, that she could note unmoved the anguish of repentance that had rendered this old man who made his tremulous confession almost beside himself with remorse ; and though tears lay too high for her to trust herself to answer him verbally, she took his hand in both of hers, with a pitying gesture, more eloquent than any form of speech.

Had Doctor Girvan been the most consummate diplomatist, instead of an honest, well-meaning, behind-the-age old man, he could not have hit on a plan better calculated to retain Grace's kindly feeling than that of a free and open confession.

After all, it is never what a person tells of himself, but what others say of him, that damages him materially. The frank plea of guilty takes the worst of the sting out of many a social as well as legal crime.

It may not be the highest nature which is ready to confess to man, but it is nevertheless the sort of nature man likes best; and whereas, had Dr. Girvan failed to take the whole of the blame on his own shoulders, she would have retained an exceeding bitter remembrance of his determined rejection of Mr. Hanlon's opinion, she never, as matters now stood, thought in the future of her father's life sacrificed as it was to old tradition, without at the same time recalling the picture of an aged man's anguished face while he in the same breath entreated her forgiveness and blamed himself for having caused her such misery.

Further, Drs. Murney and Connelley, shocked at so open a display of professional insufficiency, lack of reticence, and disregard of medical etiquette, deeming it best to make out as good a case for their fellow-practitioner as his imbecile and indiscreet revelations left possible, took immediate opportunity to efface as far as might be the impression such a direful abuse of common discretion was calculated to produce.

Between them they succeeded in sketching and filling in a very creditable series of facts founded on fiction ; that is to say, the general conclusion at which they arrived was right, though the premises on which those conclusions were founded were wrong.

The case, they assured her, was a most obscure one. How far Dr. Girvan had been right in his course of treatment they could not tell, owing to the length of time which elapsed between Mr. Moffat's attack and their own arrival ; but there was no doubt he had medical precedent of the highest authority for all he did, and if he erred, it was from no lack of

skill or prudence, but simply because nature
had chosen to clothe the complaint in a dress
similar to that worn by a totally distinct
disease; Mr. Hanlon's diagnosis of the
case might not really have been one whit more
correct than Dr. Girvan's; and finally they
assured Miss Moffat that everything which
could be done had been done, and should be
done. "If skill and attention can save him,"
said Dr. Murney "he will be spared to you."
And they left Grace, thinking they had glossed
over the little error in judgment very neatly.

Mr. Hanlon lingered behind them for a
moment. He had all a young man's enthusiasm for truth being always presented as a
nude figure, and his public experiences of
stating unpleasant facts without the slightest
atom of clothing veiling their deformity tended
undoubtedly to encourage this outspoken frankness on disagreeable topics.

For his life he could not see what good purpose the doctors proposed to effect by mystify-
ing Miss Moffat as to her father's state.

"They are raising false hopes," he thought,

and so waited to hear what remark Grace might have to make.

Doctor Murney's last words, which Dr. Connelley ratified with an approving smile, had been, " If skill and attention can save him, he will be spared to you."

" And what do you say, Mr. Hanlon ? " she asked.

" You have heard what Dr. Murney's opinion is," he answered.

" Yes, and I think I know what it is worth. The promise contained in his words will be kept to the ear and broken to the heart. Be frank with me, Mr. Hanlon ; it is so, is it not ? "

" I do not like to answer you," he said.

" But what is the use of deceiving me ? " she asked.

" None," was his answer.

" You believe, then, there is no hope ? "

" I believe nothing can save him," he said slowly. " But we will all do our best, you may be sure of that, Miss Moffat."

" Thank you," she answered. The words were nothing, but the tone in which she spoke them went straight to the surgeon's heart.

"I wish that idiot Girvan had been dead and buried rather than he should have meddled in the case," thought the surgeon. "And yet, perhaps, it is as well. A few years might have been added to this man's life, but how could he have found enjoyment in them, with the dread of THIS dogging his path? Better as it is," decided Mr. Hanlon philosophically. Like many other social reformers, his ideas about the value of life were extremely lax. The nation, the race, the world, posterity, these were the objects he desired to benefit.

What did a few or many lives matter, providing the grand result were obtained? What mattered it whether thousands died broken-hearted, if by the travail of their souls millions yet unborn tasted the delights of perfect equality of (this was a telling platform phrase, perhaps because there is no country—unless, indeed, it may be Scotland, where there is less uncovering, except amongst the beggars, than in Ireland) —"doffing their hats to no man."

Mr. Hanlon said, and doubtless thought he spoke the truth, he would cheerfully lay down his life to emancipate Ireland.

There is a considerable difference, however, between abstract propositions and actual practice. When the time came that Mr. Hanlon's chances of existence seemed jeopardized, he proved himself as solicitous to extend his days as the veriest aristocrat might have been.

Nevertheless his theories on the subject being that as a man had to die some time, it did not much matter when he died, he began after a time to consider that perhaps it was quite as well Mr. Moffat should not recover.

He had been a negative quantity ever since his arrival in Ireland. He had not done any harm, but he had not done any good. He occupied the place where a better man might stand, or which no man might advantageously fail to occupy.

A woman with money, a willing heart, an open hand, was of ten times more use in her generation than a man. Perhaps he had in his mind the old saying, "When women reign—men rule."

At any rate, he thought he could find a use for much of Miss Moffat's income, not a use so far as he personally was concerned; he was not mercenary; good things he desired, but those it was beyond the power of gold to purchase. No, he would relieve the poor, he would advance the cause, he would drive the wedge destined to split up "the dynasty of oppression," and Grace's money would help him to these ends.

She could not well now refuse to recognize him as a friend. His knowledge of society was so slight, he had not the faintest idea two such alien barks as his and hers might come nigh together, and have for a few hours a common interest and then part, "like a dream on the wide deep." He railed against society; but of its ideas, customs, habits of thought, modes of action, he was ignorant as a child.

Already he had sketched out a course of action for Grace and himself—arranged the pecuniary part she was to play in the drama, and the various modes in which her money would enable him better to enact the character he had elected to fill.

His interest, professionally, in Mr. Moffat had departed. He could do nothing for him— no one could do anything for him. He had even in the course of his limited experience beheld nature achieve triumphs of medical skill, which set science and all previous calculations utterly at nought, but his conviction was, that in this case nature meant to let matters take their course.

"She has been meddled with and thwarted," he considered ; " but for Doctor Girvan perhaps she might have had a chance, at all events we should have been left time in which to try our treatment. As matters are he is doomed. A few hours more and the master of Bayview will be wiser than the wisest man on earth. He will know more than any of us."

Which really might be considered an almost reluctant admission on the part of Mr. Hanlon's mind, not because his theology was defective, but because his self-conceit was so great, it actually touched his vanity to think a man like Mr. Moffat would know more in the next world than he knew in this.

" I have done all I could in the matter, that is certain," he said as a finish to his reflections; and Grace being in the sick-room, he went downstairs to join Drs. Murney and Connelley at breakfast.

Let death be ever so active in one place, life will be equally active in another, and the fact that the master of the house could never again welcome a guest nor issue a command did not in the smallest degree affect the appetites of the men who had come so far to strive and save him.

Doctor Girvan, indeed, saying it would choke him to "take bite or sup," had hurried home to secure a few hours' quiet before the business of the day began; but the night air and the long drive and ride, and the sharp morning air which blew crisp and cold over Bayview, sharpened the relish with which the two strange doctors looked on the well-laden table that gladdened their eyes when they entered the dining-room after their interview with Grace.

As for Mr. Hanlon, he was young; he dined early; he never supped; he did not often treat himself to the luxury of sitting up all night—in a word, breakfast was still breakfast to him, let who could not help it die, let who would live.

"A most capital cut of beef!" remarked Dr. Murney, returning from the sideboard with his plate replenished for the third time; "Connelley, let me persuade you."

"Remember I am not a sea-bird like you, and fish fresh out of the water is a treat to me. Ah! poor Moffat, how particular he used to be about the fish that came to his table!"

And the speaker shook his head and helped himself to another slice of broiled salmon.

"That was a sad mistake of Girvan's!" said Dr. Murney, looking round the room, to make sure the respectable servant who had been told they "would see to themselves" was nowhere within earshot.

"Never kept himself up with the times," explained Dr. Connelley.

"But, gentlemen," interrupted Mr. Hanlon, "if nature is always changing her diseases with the times, how is a doctor to keep himself posted up with regard to her latest ailment?"

"Nature does not change. Her diseases may be modified or extended by circumstances," said Dr. Murney, "but her laws are immutable. Science, however, finds out that diseases once classed under the same head may be separated; may be—must be; and a medical man ought to keep himself abreast of science. For instance, no doubt hundreds and thousands of persons suffering like Mr. Moffat have been treated up to quite recent times for apoplexy, and died under that treatment."

"Pleasant!" ejaculated Mr. Hanlon.

"Inevitable," said Dr. Connelley, with philosophical composure. And after all he was right; the knowledge of those days would be deemed ignorance now.

"I will drive over to-morrow," remarked Dr. Murney, who, having finished his breakfast, was drawing on his gloves preparatory to that return journey which was to be made once again in Mr. Moffat's tax-cart, with one of Mr. Moffat's horses. "Although indeed—" the pause was as significant as the words.

"And I will come too, if I can," added Dr. Connelley; "but I am afraid—" once again an ellipsis, which Mr. Hanlon filled up at his discretion.

"I suppose you will watch the case?" suggested Dr. Murney.

"With Girvan? yes. He and I had a quarrel last night, but I will not desert the poor old fellow now."

"Ah, well, you need not fear having to wait long for the end," observed Dr. Connelley. "It is a question of hours. He may be alive when we come to-morrow—but I think myself he cannot last out the day."

"He will go with the first or second ebb tide, I should say," corrected Dr. Murney; "most likely the second. Certainly I should say not the third."

There was one question Mr. Hanlon wanted to ask before they left.

"No doubt," he began, "Miss Moffat will wish to send for the rector; if she does, what am I to say?"

Dr. Murney took a pinch of snuff and looked at Dr. Connelley. Dr. Connelley looked out of the window and made no sign.

"I think," answered the former uneasily, I should let her send for the rector, and explain the position to him."

"Precisely. But what is the position? He will never be conscious again."

"In this world," amended Dr. Connelley.

"In this world," repeated Dr. Murney, taking off his hat as if he were in a church.

There was a moment's respectful silence. Then said Dr. Murney, as if he conceived affairs which strictly speaking belonged to the clergy had been encroached upon by him,—

"Of course, Mr. Hanlon, had Dr. Connelley and I considered there was the remotest chance of a restoration to consciousness, we should at once have advised Miss Moffat to send for her father's attorney."

With which utterance Dr. Murney took his leave.

"So it is," thought Mr. Hanlon, after he had seen Dr. Connelley mounted and answered his farewell wave of the hand; "So it is; the law first—God after."

Till the great assize is over, who may tell how these apparent incongruities shall be settled; how the toil and trouble a man often entails on those who are to come after is quite compatible with a quiet death-bed and the rules of eternal justice!

To me it has always seemed that the person who, having time and inclination to make his peace with Heaven, as the not inappropriate phrase has it, makes that peace, and leaves mundane affairs to conduct themselves, must have failed in his worldly trust, must have neglected to put out at interest some of those talents with which he was entrusted.

In my poor opinion the doctors were right, and Mr. Hanlon wrong. A man, to all ordinary ways of thinking, ought not to be able to turn his eyes with a steady gaze heavenward so long as there is anything on earth demanding his attention, and yet it may be that when the supreme moment has arrived, and this world is vanishing, and another opening, it may be then, I say, that not merely do the most important projects of this life dwarf into insignificance, but that a glimpse is caught of that perfect faith which enables its possessor to leave the welfare of the nearest and dearest to him in higher hands than those of man.

Upon no other supposition does it appear to me possible to account for the supine selfishness with which those who have worldly goods to leave sometimes fold their hands and remain tranquil, whilst five minutes devoted to temporal matters might save miseries and heartburnings untold.

Mr. Hanlon's speech, however, was prompted quite as much by the spirit of opposition as of religion. Had the other doctors suggested sending for a clergyman, he would most

probably have mentally sneered at " old women
who believed in the efficacy of a death-bed
repentance."

" Show me how a man lived, and I will tell
you how he died," was one of his favourite
quotations ; and yet now, when he came face to
face with a death which allowed no instant of
preparation, he could not help admitting—he
was not the advanced Republican of these
times, recollect—there must be something in
the almost universal desire human beings feel
to be permitted to linger, if only for a few
minutes, on the shores of that mighty ocean
which washes on the one side the fair land of
life, and on the other the hidden mysteries of
eternity.

So far as Mr. Moffat's temporal affairs were
concerned, he had left nothing to be settled in
a hurry at the last hour of his existence. In
the methodical, self-contained life he had led
there was no sign to indicate the manner of
death he should die. Probably he himself
never imagined for a moment he should be
called upon to leave this world except in the
most orderly and usual manner.

Nevertheless his affairs were in perfect order. All the attorneys and accountants in Ireland could not have put them in more intelligible shape.

Concerning other matters, who could tell? Himself and his Maker alone knew how far the peremptory summons found him ready to leave a world which had always been a pleasant one to the owner of Bayview.

The clergyman was sent for and came, but it all turned out as Dr. Murney had predicted.

The tide ebbed, and the tide flowed; when it ebbed again his soul set forth on a longer and more awful voyage than mortal mariner ever undertook.

Little more than thirty hours had passed since Grace walked slowly homeward from the Lone Rock, and yet the whole current and colour of her life was changed. The sunbeams danced merrily on the waters, the sea rippled in once more upon the shore, the trees and shrubs shook out their green foliage, and the air was almost heavy with the rich perfumes of summer. In the distance the hills seemed almost to melt into the soft blue of the sky. Everywhere there was beauty, and gladness, and sunshine, but Grace saw nothing of the beauty, felt nothing of the gladness. Over the house there brooded the shadow of mighty wings, for the angel of death had paused in his flight; one whose voice had been so suddenly stilled lay silent within; he who had been master there might dwell in that pleasant abode —never more.

CHAPTER II.

SAYING GOOD-BYE.

THE summer was gone and early autumn had come before Grace Moffat walked beyond the precincts of Bayview. Sorrow not sickness had kept her solitary. With the bitterness of her grief she could not endure friends or strangers to meddle, and so all alone she bore the first brunt of her trouble, all alone she formed her plans, rooted up the old projects and fanciful aims of her past life, and, spite of her former convictions on the subject of absenteeism, determined to leave Ireland, if not for ever, at all events for a considerable period.

In truth, without sacrificing her liberty she could not well have remained there.

Although in the eyes of Kingslough she was fast verging towards the sere and yellow leaf period of life, she was not old enough to set Mrs. Grundy at defiance and reside at Bayview without a duenna, and that was an encumbrance Grace had no desire to burden herself with. Further, she knew that every eligible man within reach would rush to offer her consolation in the first instance, and his hand in the second; and that mothers would outvie each other in offering to supply a father's place to so eligible a daughter-in-law as herself.

She was of course a much more desirable investment in the matrimonial market than had been the case during her father's lifetime. All he once possessed was hers now unreservedly; and amongst men in search of rich wives, the increased value of Miss Moffat's hand might readily have been computed by a rule-of-three sum.

All this Grace felt bitterly. Now when she wanted a friend as she had never wanted one before, she found herself surrounded by those who all, she suspected, held a second purpose concealed behind their kindly advances.

Perhaps she wronged the impulses of many a warm heart by this idea, but money was an article truly needed at that time amongst the Irish gentry. Heiresses were scarce, encumbered estates numerous. So to speak, the bulk of the old families were in a state of insolvency, and driven to their wits' ends to avert the final catastrophe which the famine only precipitated, which it alone certainly never could have induced amongst an aristocracy already tottering to the verge of ruin.

How were the heirs of impoverished estates covered with debt as with a garment to mend their position except by marriage?

Every profession was overstocked; they could not go into trade. Even had they possessed the requisite ability necessary to carry on a business successfully, the prejudices of the country must have deterred them from attempting to mend matters by a move in that direction.

A few went to India, where some succeeded and others died. Australia and the West Indies absorbed most of the adventurous or speculative youth of the period. In Australia they led a not disagreeable life, spite of hardships they certainly never could have endured at home. In the West Indies success resolved itself into a game at hazard with death. If death won, why they died, and there was an end of it; if they won, they won wealth as well.

For the male gentry who remained at home on the ancestral acres, there were but two courses open. One to marry a girl without money, and so hasten the advent of ruin; the other to marry a girl with money, and so defer to another generation that bankruptcy which it was impossible could be averted for ever.

In such a state of society the woman herself counted for very little. Love matches were made, it is true, every day, and resulted in a good deal of domestic unhappiness, pinching, saving, meanness, and an infinite number of children; but in those cases where love and prudence might have been supposed able to travel together, prudence turned love out of court, and no heiress, let her be as good and beautiful as she pleased, could make quite sure whether it were she who was being wooed, or the comfortable thousands the care and affection of some exceptionally fortunate ancestor had saved for her benefit.

Had she been deaf, humpbacked, lame, afflicted with a squint, eighty years of age, an heiress need not have despaired of attracting suitors.

When sons were shy or indifferent, when they seemed inclined to balk, as a hunting gentleman described their reluctance to go wooing, mothers courted sometimes not unsuccessfully in their stead; and had Grace been one of the blood royal, she could scarcely have had greater attention showered upon her than was the case once the funeral was over and the terms of her father's will known.

But to visitors Grace sedulously denied herself; invitations she steadily refused to accept, with the exception of one which she took time to consider.

It came from Mrs. Hartley, and was couched in these words:—

" I have been thinking much about you and

your position, and putting my own selfish wishes on one side, really and truly believe the best thing you can do is to come to me for a time.   If you stay where you are you will be driven to marry some one.   The day must come when in utter weariness of saying 'No,' you will say 'Yes;' not because you care much for the suitor, or he is especially eligible, but because you feel one husband is preferable to a host of lovers.

"We shall not bore each other; you shall go your way, and I shall continue on mine.

"We will travel if you like; I shall not herald your arrival amongst my friends in the character of an heiress, be sure of that.   I have no pet young man free of the house to whom I wish to see you married.   Come and try the experiment, at all events.   If you still preserve your Utopian ideas on the subject of Ireland's regeneration, it may be as well for you, before you begin the work, to see that the inhabitants of another country really manage to keep their doorsteps white—and their children's hair combed without the intervention of philanthropists like yourself, or demagogues like Mr. Hanlon. By the way, I hope you are not getting entangled in that quarter.

" No doubt the young man is clever, and behaved well at the time of your poor father's attack; but still, these are no reasons why he should marry your father's daughter.

" *It would not do*, Grace. If by your marriage to such a man you were able to ensure a meat dinner every day to all the tenant farmers in Ireland, you would find even that desirable result dearly purchased at the cost of so unsuitable an alliance. I do you the justice to feel certain your heart is unaffected, but the circumstances have been propitious for touching your fancy; and I know of old what a snare that lively imagination you possess is capable of proving.

" Talking of imagination, what has become of the handsome hero of your teens? What has he done? What is he doing? I see the young earl is dead; and I understand that where the sapling fell it is to lie, as the means of the family do not permit of a second grand funeral within so short a time.   Opinions here are divided as to the chances of Mr. Robert Somerford succeeding to the title.

" Some persons say the new earl is privately married and has a family, others that he will marry, others that he is and has always been single, that he has one foot in the grave and will shortly have another in likewise.   It is a case in which I should decline to advise if you asked my opinion.

" If you marry Robert Somerford he may be Earl of Glendare.   If you wait till he is Earl of Glendare, you may never be Countess of Glendare.   And indeed I shall not desire to see you raised to the peerage.   I do not think greatness would sit easily upon your shoulders. I believe you would be far happier married to some honest, honourable man in our own rank of life than you could be amongst the nobility. But there is no honest, honourable young man in our own rank of life residing near here whose cause I wish to plead, so you will be quite safe in coming to me.   Will you *think* the matter over and come ? "

Which letter Grace, after having thought the matter over, answered in these words : —

"I will go to you. Amongst all the people I know, there is no one I trust so fully, I believe in so implicitly as I do in you. I will let Bayview furnished. I will set my affairs in order, and leave the dear old place which has grown hateful to me—temporarily only, I hope—for I should like, when I have advanced sufficiently in age, to wear caps, and set the world's opinions at defiance, to return to Ireland, and spend my declining years and my income amongst mine ' ain folk.'

"Were I a stronger-minded woman, I suppose I should be able to conquer my grief and defy public criticism by starting on what you would call a career of philanthropy ; but sorrow and the world, this little world of Kingslough, are, I confess, too much for me. As you say, I believe I should marry out of mere weariness of spirit.

" My pensioners I shall leave to Mrs. Larkin, who will rejoice in seeing the poor crowd round her door like robins in the winter.

"If anything were capable of making me laugh now, I should laugh at your idea of there being the slightest tender feeling between me and Mr. Hanlon. It is because by some nameless instinct I comprehend he never could by any chance care for me that I have seen more of him since my irreparable loss than has been perhaps, situated as I am, quite wise. I do not mean that he has called here often, or that I have chanced to meet him more than two or three times in my solitary walks by the seashore ; but still you know what all small places are, what this small place is especially.

"Kingslough has talked, is talking—Kingslough says my head is turned, and that I am bent on flinging myself and my money away on a man who, some say—you remember Kingslough was always remarkable for its vehemence of expression, 'should be drummed out of the town '—and others think worthy of being—do not faint at the phrase, it is not mine—'strung up.'

"I have told you that I am positive Mr. Hanlon has no intention, even for the weal of the nation, of ever asking me to marry him ; and yet I have an uneasy conviction he has some purpose to serve in cultivating better relations between us, which purpose I cannot at present divine. Moreover, I fear he has not given so direct a denial to those rumours which have bracketed his name and mine in such an undesirable connection as I think, were I a man, I should have done under similiar circumstances. Kingslough says positively I have lost my heart and my senses—of the state of both you will be able to judge when we meet.

"Mr. Robert Somerford has at length given me the opportunity of refusing the honour of allying myself to the house of Glendare. I am glad of this, for I should scarcely have liked to leave Bayview whilst a chance remained of his doing so. He is handsomer than ever—years only improve his appearance ; but were he beautiful as Adonis he could never be my hero more.

" He was first sentimental and sympathetic, next pressing in his entreaties, and sceptical as to the genuineness of my 'No.' Lastly he was insolent and made as much of himself and his position as though he had been nursed in the lap of royalty, and lived all his life on terms of equality with kings and queens. Familiarity may in my case have bred contempt, but I certainly never in the days when I admired him most considered he was so much my superior as appears is the case.

"I was equal, however, to the emergency; my desolate position, and my heavy mourning, the sorrow I have passed through, all combine to give me a courage I lacked in former times.

"Whilst he was still exalting himself and depreciating me—reciting the glories of the Glendares and contrasting the rank to which he could have raised me with the level of obscurity in which my refusal doomed me to remain for life, maundering on as one might have thought only an angry ill-bred woman or a spoiled child could have maundered—I rose and rang the bell.

"'Perhaps you will go now, Mr. Somerford,' I said, ruthlessly cutting across a sentence in which he was drawing a picture of my future life when married to a poor apothecary who had not even the recommendation of being possessed of all his senses. 'Perhaps you will go now, and spare yourself the vexation of being asked to leave before a servant.'

" I never saw a man so taken by surprise. He got up, made me a low, mocking bow, and quitted the room without uttering another word.

" Next time he asks any one to marry him, he says, he will take care the lady is in his own rank of life.

" He had been gradually provoking me, so at that point I broke silence and suggested the advisability of his ascertaining at the same time whether her worldly means were as excellent as his own.

" You will blame me for this, of course ; but if I had bitten back the words they would have choked me.

" There was a time when I could have married him, and probably repented doing so every hour of my after life. I told him this, and he pressed me much to say when my feelings underwent so great a change.

" 'On that day,' I answered, 'when you forced me to remark,—We had made you welcome at Bayview, and we now make you welcome to stay away.'

" It is only women with money, I fancy, who have to endure impertinence at the hands of their suitors. I suppose the fact is a feeling of tenderness for the beloved one mingles even with the bitterness of losing her ; but the wildest fancy cannot suppose any feeling of tenderness towards a fortune that a man sees plainly can never be possessed by him.

" Every obstacle to my accepting your invitation is now removed.

" Our servants seem determined to celebrate the event of their master's death with a series of weddings. He left them each a sum of money which, though it would appear little to English people of the same rank, is wealth to them, and a number of alliances have been arranged on the strength of these legacies which would have amused you had you seen the match-making in progress.

" On the whole, I am inclined to think that

even in Ireland the possession of a nest egg produces the same effect upon human beings as it does upon a hen. A desire to lay another beside it becomes at once irresistible. After that remark you will not be surprised to hear the marriages in this establishment are chiefly remarkable for prudence. Jane, the dairy-maid, is going to invest her money in cows, and a husband who owns a small cottage, the right of grazing over a large tract of common land, and a cabbage-garden, in which he pro-poses to erect byres. The cook, whom you may perhaps remember for the excellence of her omelets and the warmth of her temper, clubs her legacy with that of the coachman, and they intend to take a public-house five miles down the coast, and add posting to the business. I will not weary you with further matrimonial details.

"The youngest and prettiest of the establish-ment, my own little maid, takes her money, supplemented by a gift from me, back to her sickly mother.

"'I shall be able to stay with her always

now, Miss Grace,' she said, crying and laughing in the same breath. 'I know enough, thanks be to you, to teach a little school, and we'll be happy as the day is long.'

"I have spoken to no one concerning my own plans; though of course every one knows I am going to leave Bayview, no person suspects that I intend to visit England.

"It has indeed been stated that I mean to spend the winter abroad with Lady Glendare. Her ladyship sent me a very civil note, favoured by Mrs. Dillwyn, saying how grieved she was to hear of my bereavement, speaking of her own loss, and adding that, if I thought a thorough change would prove beneficial to my health and spirits, she would be delighted if I would visit her.

"Which was very kind, particularly from a member of a family famous for the shortness of their memories of favours received.

"This, I conclude, gave rise to the first report, which has now, however, been superseded by another. I am going to stay with Mr. Hanlon's mother, who is to come so far as Dublin to meet me!

"I mean to-day to bid good-bye to the Scotts; to-morrow, the next day, and the next, I shall employ in paying farewell visits and in gratifying the curiosity of my friends. Can you not fancy the entreaties with which I shall be assailed to stay in my own country and amongst my own people? My father's solicitor is delighted with the proposal that he and his family shall occupy Bayview for the autumn. He will endeavour to let it from November next.

"I shall break my journey at Dublin, from which place I will write to you again; but under any circumstances I hope to be talking to you face to face within a fortnight from the present time."

And having sealed and despatched this letter, Grace, as has been stated, for the first time since her father's death left behind her the grounds of Bayview, and wended her way towards the Castle Farm.

With a feeling of sick surprise she paused when she reached the top of the divisional road and looked at the fields to right and left. The meadows were still uncut; acres of long rich grass had been laid by the rain, trampled by the cattle. The potato blossoms had flowered and faded; the potato apples were beginning to turn brown on the stems, but not a spade had been put in to dig the roots out of the ground.

In the other lands lying around she saw hayricks; she beheld men busy at work; she heard the voices of the women and children who were almost playing at their labour, so rejoiced were all hearts to find the heavy crop the upturned earth disclosed; but at the Castle Farm there was no sign of toil or of gladness.

There was a dead stillness about the place which told Grace the beginning of the end had begun. Spite of the rich grass thick with clover, spite of the wealth lying buried in the broad ridges of the potato fields, spite of the luxuriance of the ripening corn, she knew ruin was sitting by the once hospitable hearth, stealthily biding its time till it should turn husband and wife and children out of house and home upon the world.

No active signs of grief—no outbreak of

sorrow could have affected Grace like the dumb testimony which gave evidence of the crisis that had come.

When before, in hay-time, had Amos and his boys and his men not been up at the first streak of light, in order to get well on with their labour before the sun gaining power— and the dews drying off the grass—made mowing weary work ?

When had the potatoes ever lain in the ground as they were lying now ? when had not all needful tasks been expedited and got well out of hand before the time came for the ingathering of the corn ?

Miss Moffat's eyes filled with tears as she looked at the deserted fields that had borne their increase only to point more forcibly the ruin which was come to the Castle Farm.

If she had seen a sale going on in the place ; had she beheld a crowd of strangers in the yard, and heard a babel of tongues in the air ; had the horses and the cows and the busy fussing hens, and the fat well-to-do pigs been taken away while she looked, the scene could scarcely have struck her with the numb dread that for a time paralysed her steps.

Then it all came upon her. They had sown, but they might not reap; they had planted, but they might not gather; on the land they had held so long they were tres-passers, and if they still remained in the old homestead it was only because there is nothing more difficult than to get rid of people who have determined to remain.

Amos Scott had so determined; but the law was closing him in slowly, surely.

It was eating his substance first; while he had a pound in the traditional stocking, or the ability to borrow a pound—while he had a shoe to his foot and a shirt to his back, it refrained from cutting short his torture, but once let the cruise fail, and the law would scourge him with scorpions out of that once happy garden which never again might seem like paradise to Amos or one of his family.

Out of the sunlight Grace passed into the house, where, by reason of the glare from which she had come, she could at first scarcely distinguish any object; but after a second or two she beheld Mrs. Scott, aged and haggard, who, in her hands holding a coat of her husband's she had been engaged in patching, rose and bade her visitor welcome.

She was quite alone; a rare thing in that populous house. Inside as out the same stillness prevailed, a stillness like unto the Egyptian darkness, inasmuch as it could be felt.

The first words uttered were by Mrs. Scott, in sympathy for Miss Moffat's affliction; but Grace, though her burden seemed heavy, knew the dead had no need of help or remembrance, and here face to face with her was at least one human being who had.

"Tell me about yourselves," she said, passing her handkerchief across the large soft eyes that would encourage tears to shelter themselves under the white lids and long lashes. "We cannot do anything more for *him*. It was a great shock. I sometimes seem as if I were unable to realize it even yet; but it is true, and I must learn to bear the greatest trouble God sends one of his creatures."

" The greatest, Miss ? " said Mrs. Scott in-
quiringly ; she was sympathetic and respectful,
but she could not quite fall in with this opinion.

She had her trouble, and if she heard that
the trouble of another might be greater, who
shall blame her for being slow of belief.

There cannot be much doubt that the man
who has broken his leg feels sceptical when
told that his next neighbour who has broken
his ankle is in worse case than he. As a matter of theory, people may sympathize with the
griefs of their fellow-creatures, but as a matter
of fact the only sorrows which are ever thoroughly understood are those a man has himself to bear ; and this is reasonable enough, re-
membering that after the lapse of even a short
time, a man finds it difficult to recall vividly
the anguish and the shame and the agony he
may once have been obliged to pass through.

Mrs. Scott's pain was very present with her,
however, on that beatiful morning. She was
in the midst of a trouble which might well
have exhausted a more patient woman. She
had to sit still and see her household gods

broken one by one; she was forced, as she said herself, to "bide quiet" whilst ruin stalked towards their home, drawing nearer every hour. Death to her seemed naturally a less trial than this lengthened torture, and she could not agree with her visitor when Miss Moffat answered,—

"The greatest because it is hopeless."

"Not making light of your trouble, Miss Grace, don't you think it may be just as hopeless a grief as death to feel yourself coming to want and your children to beggary ?"

"If there were no way to avert such misfortunes, perhaps not," was the reply; "but it is because we cannot avert death, because we can never hope in this world to see those who are gone, that I say death is so terrible a grief."

"It is terrible," Mrs. Scott agreed; "but I don't feel as if it was as hard a sorrow as to see everything going, and not be able to put out a finger to save us from ruin. There are the potatoes undug in the ground, and I dursn't take up a root of them to boil for the dinner.

We have had to sell the cows, for we were
" threatened " if we tried to graze them.   The
boys have nothing to do, and the meadows are
all laid; but they warned Amos off when he
went to mow.   They poisoned our dog because
he flew at one of the bailiffs Brady sent ; and
they tell me now Brady is going to get the
grass in, and the potatoes up, and the corn cut
when it ripens, if he has to bring a regiment
of soldiers to protect his men."

At the idea of which imposing array Mrs.
Scott dropped her work on her knee, heaved a
deep sigh, and remarked,—

" God alone knows what the end will be ! "

" I will tell you what the end ought to
be," said Grace kindly.   " You ought to begin
to pack up your belongings now, and leave the
Castle Farm as soon as ever you can get out
of it."

" Amos'll never leave it alive," she answered.   " He is not a hard man to talk to in
a general way, but Brady has tried to head
him, and it has made him that dour, there is
no reasoning with him."

"Have you ever really tried to reason with him?" Miss Moffat inquired.

"Not at first, I'll own it. I was as keen on as himself for fighting to the last; but, oh! Miss Grace, when the trouble comes inside the door, it is the woman feels it. She must hold up and have a bite for the men folks to eat if her heart is just breaking; and I'm fairly tired of it. I feel I'd be that glad to creep into any hole where we could be quiet, I couldn't tell you."

"Where is Amos?" asked her visitor, after a pause.

"Gone to Glenwellan to see the lawyer; now we have sold Tom he has to walk there and back every step of the way. He is spending his all in law, Miss Grace. Shure the very money I got for the hens and the ducks and the other cratures he made me give him, and me saving it for the time when we'll want it sorely."

"What does Amos hope to do?" inquired Grace. "What does he expect the lawyers can do for him?"

"That's beyond me to tell. He wants his rights, and he says he'll have them."

"What are his rights?"

"Oh, that's easy telling; this place he paid the renewal of."

"I am going away,—" began Grace, with apparent irrelevance.

"So I heard tell," interpolated Mrs. Scott.

"And before I go I want to put this matter before you clearly, as I see it; as others, wiser and more capable than I, see it also."

"Yes, Miss," said Mrs. Scott in a tone which implied that Grace might talk and she herself might listen, but that her opinions would remain the same.

And indeed is this not always the case? Is it not always when talking and listening are signally useless that opinions alter?

"Supposing," said Grace, a little fluttered by reason of her own boldness, "I went to Dublin and said I must have a new piano."

"Likely you will some day," agreed Mrs. Scott, as her visitor paused for a moment and hesitated.

"And suppose for the sake of argument," went on Grace, "I decided to spend a hundred pounds."

"It would be a heap of money," commented her auditor.

"Or fifty, or twenty," said Miss Moffat, seeing her mistake; "say twenty pounds; and that I chose a piano and told the man where to send it, and paid him the money and took no receipt for it. After I leave, another person sees the same piano, likes it, pays the money, and gets a receipt. Shortly I begin to wonder why the instrument is not sent home, and I write to the seller. I receive an answer saying he is dead, and that no one knows anything about the matter except that the piano I mention has been sold and delivered to Mr. So-and-so. Now such a case would be undoubtedly a hard one for me, but I should never think of throwing good money after bad in trying to put spilt milk back into a basin; and yet this is what Amos persists in attempting. Do you understand what I mean?"

"You speak very clever, Miss Grace," was the reply.

"I am afraid I do not speak at all cleverly," said her visitor. "I wish any words of mine could persuade Amos and you how utterly useless it is for you to continue the resistance he has begun."

"Would you have him give up everything, then, Miss, and see us turned out on the world —we who have always tried to keep decent and respectable as you know, Miss Grace?"

"I do know," was the answer, "but I see no help for it—if a thing has to be done at last, it may as well and better be done at first."

"I am thinking Amos will fight it to the end," said Mrs. Scott calmly,

"But what folly it is!" exclaimed Miss Moffat.

"Like enough; I wouldn't be so ill bred as to contradict you, Miss, even if I could."

"But it is impossible you can be happy or comfortable living in this sort of way."

"Happy, comfortable," repeated the poor woman, then added with sudden vehemence, "And who is it that has made us unhappy and uncomfortable, but that villain Brady ? It'll come home to him though ; sure as sure, Miss Grace, it will. We may not live to see it, but the day will come that others will mind what Brady done to us and say, 'Serve him right,' no matter what trouble is laid upon him."

"But you do not wish any harm to happen to him?" suggested Grace, who, having no personal feud with Mr. Brady, naturally felt shocked at Mrs. Scott's bitterness of expression.

"Don't I?" retorted the woman. "It would be blessed news if one came in now and said, 'Brady is lying stiff and stark out in the field yonder.'"

"Hush, hush, hush!" entreated Grace, laying her hand on the lean unlovely arm which had once been plump and comely. "Oh! I wish I could talk to you as I want to talk. I wish I could say good things as other people are able. I wish I could persuade you to bear your heavy burden patiently, feeling certain God in His own good time will lighten it for you. I cannot think there is any reality in religion if it does not support us in trials like these, and you are a religious woman, dear Mrs. Scott. I remember, as if it was yesterday, the Bible stories you used to tell me when I was a bit of a thing wearing mourning for the first time."

Mrs. Scott's face began to work, then her eyes filled with tears, then one slowly trickled down her cheek, which she wiped away with the corner of her checked apron, then with a catching sob, she said,—

"Ay, those were brave days, Miss Grace, brave, heartsome days. It was easy to feel good and Christian-like then, and wish well to everybody; but I can't do it now, I cannot. When I'm sitting here all alone, texts come into my head; but they are all what I used to call bad ones, about vengeance, and hatred, and punishment. There are no others I can mind now. That thief of the world has destroyed us body and soul, but it will come to him. He will get his deserts yet."

Grace rose, and walked into an inner room, where, on the top of a chest of drawers, bright as beeswax could keep them, lay the family

Bible, with Scott's spectacles, heirlooms like the book, reposing upon it.

Lifting the Bible she carried it out, placed it upon the dresser, and, turning to the Gospels, read the last six verses of the fifth chapter of St. Matthew softly and slowly. Then she closed the volume and took it back again.

" It's well for them that can do all that," said Mrs. Scott, not defiantly, but in simple good faith.

" Some day we shall all be able to feel it, and do it, please God," answered Grace, and, stooping over the back of Mrs. Scott's chair, she kissed the face of the humble friend who had once been like a mother to her.

" Good-bye," she said. " Let Reuben write to me, and get Amos away from here, if you can, before worse comes of it."

" What is this, Miss Grace ? " asked Mrs. Scott, as her visitor laid a small packet in her lap.

" It is what you will need," said Grace, " when perhaps I am not near at hand to come to for it."

E 2

" Is it money ? " inquired the woman.

" Yes; surely you do not mind taking it from me ? "

" No, I wouldn't mind. There aren't many I could ask to help us, or that I could take help from; but I am not that high in my turn I'd refuse it from you. Take it with you though, Miss Grace. Don't leave it here. I could not keep it secret from the good man— we have never had anything separate, and he'd either be angry with me for taking it, or else he'd want it to spend on the law."

" In that case I will not leave it," said Grace emphatically ; " only remember this one thing,—whilst I am alive and have a pound, you need never want. Bid me good-bye now, for I must go."

" Good-bye," answered Mrs. Scott, taking Grace's hand in her own, after carefully wiping the latter on her apron; " God send you safe to England and back again ! " and with this customary form of farewell, which, familiar as it is to those resident in Ireland, always strikes solemnly on the ear, Mrs. Scott suffered her visitor to depart, watching her retreating figure till it was lost to sight, and then returning to her seat and her occupation.

"And back again!" Grace repeated to herself, as she looked over the glory of land and water—hill and wood lying calm and beautiful under a flood of golden sunshine. "And back again! what will have happened, I wonder, by the time I return?"

CHAPTER III.

BREAKING THE ICE.

WERE I to say that at first Miss Moffat neither admired the country nor liked the people of England, I should only be expressing the sentiments of an entire nation in the person of a single individual; other people may have met with Irish men and Irish women who took kindly to Saxon soil on the first intention, but for my own part I have still to see the recently imported Celt willing to admit there can be any good thing found in the land.

It is very curious to consider how rapidly educated English tourists take to Ireland—to the inhabitants, the brogue, the scenery, the whisky—and then to contrast with this the length of time required to acclimatize an Irish person of any rank to England and English ways. Safely, I think, it may be asserted that there is nothing on this side the channel, from the red-tiled roofs of picturesque old barns to the glories of the Row, which finds favour in Hibernian eyes. They may like England at last—many do—but they never like it at first.

To this rule Grace formed no exception. There was nothing she liked in the foreign land to which she had voluntarily exiled herself. Amongst her own country people, she even fancied Mrs. Hartley had changed, and changed for the worse, from the decided, incisive widow, whose tongue had been the terror and whose dress had been the envy of feminine Kingslough.

She was more conventional and less amusing, the young lady considered; but Mrs. Hartley's latest surroundings presented no temptations to unconventionality, and it would have been extremely difficult to prove herself clever at the expense of the eminently dull and decorous people amongst whom her lot was now cast.

The style in which her friend lived was also at first a trial to Grace.

The extreme simplicity of her own bringing up—the modesty of the Bayview establishment —the unpretending fashion of receiving and visiting that at one time obtained in Ireland rendered the rules and ceremonies of—to quote Mrs. Hartley—"a more advanced civilization" irksome in the extreme to a person who had from her childhood upwards been accustomed to an exceptional freedom of action; whilst after the inoffensive familiarity of Irish servants, the formality and decorum of Mrs. Hartley's highly-trained domestics seemed cold and heartless.

In a word, Miss Grace was more than slightly home-sick; in all probability, had she possessed a home to go back to, she would have received some early communication compelling her to return to Ireland.

All of this, or at least much of this, so

shrewd a woman as Mrs. Hartley could not fail to notice; she had expected the desire to manifest itself, though not exactly so violently, and she was accordingly quite prepared to let it run its course without much interference from her.

It was not in her nature, however, to refrain altogether from a little raillery on the subject.

"The cakes and the ales of this gormandizing land will find favour in your eyes some day, Grace," she remarked. "I do not despair of hearing you confess other forms of diet may be as appetizing as milk and potatoes."

"I can fancy many things more appetizing than potatoes as boiled in England," Miss Moffat would retort, not without some slight sign of irritation. Her temper was not quite so sweet, Mrs. Hartley noticed, as had been the case formerly.

"She will not make an amiable old maid," considered her friend. "As she gets on in life her wine will turn to vinegar; she is the kind of woman who ought to have a husband and half-a-dozen children, to prevent her growing morbid and disagreeable—like all other philanthropists, she has had some serious disappointments, and I must say they have not improved her. She ought to marry; but, like her, I confess I cannot imagine who the happy man is to be. Beauty, wealth, amiability! she has the three gifts men value most, and yet it seems to me that not a man suitable in any solitary respect has ever yet asked her to be his wife—except John Riley. I wonder what he would think of her now? Who could have imagined she would ever have developed into so lovely a creature?"

There were two things by which Mrs. Hartley set great store — competence and beauty.

Poor people and ugly people were to her as repellent as many diseases. Genteel poverty was one of her abhorrences, plain faces another; and it may therefore be imagined that when she found two most desirable advantages combined in one human being, she gave way to exultation so perfectly frank that it struck Grace with amazement.

" What a beautiful creature you are ! " she said as, Grace seated beside her in the carriage, they drove along the level English roads to Mrs. Hartley's house.

" I am not very beautiful now, I am afraid," answered Miss Moffat ; " tired, burnt up with the sun and the wind, and smothered with dust, I feel utterly ashamed of my appearance."

" Ah ! well you need not be, my dear. I always thought you would grow up very pretty, but certainly I never expected to see you so pretty as you are. What do the Kingslough oracles think of Gracie Moffat now ? "

" The Kingslough oracles disapprove of my being personally presentable," Grace answered. " They likewise think it a pity that, if I were designed to be good-looking, good looks were not conferred upon me in my youth. Further, they consider that as I have plenty of money, I ought to be plain ; and, besides all this, they think I am not so particularly good-looking after all."

" The dear Kingslough !   It is like a dream of old times to hear its opinions summed up so concisely."

" I wonder what Kingslough would think of your present state of magnificence," said Grace, a little mischievously.   " If you were to drive through Kingslough in this carriage, you would have the whole town out, and furnish conversation for a month."

Mrs. Hartley laughed, but her mirth was a little forced; she did not like her splendour dimmed by the breath of ridicule, but she was too much a woman of the world to show her annoyance.

" When we are in Turkey we do as the Turkeys do, to borrow a phrase from one of your own countrymen," she answered.   " If any adverse wind stranded me to-morrow in Ireland, I should at once purchase a jaunting-car and advertise for a Protestant without incumbrance, able to drive and wait at table."

Miss Moffat remembered   that when   the

speaker was stranded in Kingslough she dispensed even with the jaunting-car ; but Mrs. Hartley had so neatly hit off the popular method of proceeding, that Grace, tired as she was, and feeling rather lonely and miserable, thought that silence might be wisdom, and refrained from reminding her friend of the dreary drives they had taken in that particular style of conveyance which the young lady detested.

"Besides," went on Mrs. Hartley, as though guessing at her companion's thoughts. " I am now a much richer woman than I was in those days. Money has come to me as it generally does to people who have it. Gold has a way of attracting gold which is certainly very remarkable. I used to think my income was as large as I should care to have it, but since more has been added I find I can manage to spend it very comfortably."

This scrap of conversation may be taken as samples of many which followed. Mrs. Hartley and her guest talked, walked, drove, paid visits together, but they did not at once fall into the old familiar relations that had formerly been so pleasant.

In effect both were different persons from the young heiress and the rich English widow of Grace's genial spring-time; and even if they had not so changed, it is a difficult matter to take up, after years of separation, the thread of a friendship at the precise point where it was dropped, and go on weaving the many-coloured web of intimate association as though nothing had occurred to stop its progress.

Besides this, that which Grace styled " Mrs. Hartley's magnificence " was not a thing this country-bred maiden could accustom herself to in a moment.

Hers was a model property; small, it is true, but maintained as Grace had never seen any place maintained before, unless indeed it might be a botanical garden. Not half so large as Bayview, a very doll's house and toy grounds in comparison with those of Woodbrook! but the order which kept the lawns trimmed, the hedges clipped, the walks rolled, the house from garret to cellar a marvel of comfort and luxury, was enough to make a thoughtful and devoted Irishwoman like Grace ask herself a few very awkward questions, and make her feel for the moment angry because she could not avoid a sensation of shame at the contrast suggested.

"I wish I could ever hope to be so admirable a manager in all respects as you are, Mrs. Hartley," said Grace one day, after she had heard that lady issue some rather peremptory commands to her head gardener.

"One cannot be a handsome young thing like you and a sharp old busybody like myself," replied Mrs. Hartley, not displeased, however, at the compliment; "and then remember I was born and brought up in a country where order is Heaven's first law; in a land where it is the fashion to keep the doorsteps white, it is natural that one should like to see one's own steps presentable. There is a great deal in habit. Although in the abstract no doubt you admire English order and cleanliness, still I have no doubt but that in your heart of hearts you think we are fussy and over-particular.

Miss Moffat laughed and coloured.

"To be quite frank," she replied, "I like the result produced, but I do not like the means by which it is produced. Perpetual hearthstoning and rolling, and mowing and cutting and clipping produce marvellous effects, I confess; but still I think the constant recurrence of such days of small things must tend to dwarf the intellect and make life seem a very poor affair."

"Irish, my dear, very; but these are opinions about which there is no use arguing. I should have considered begging in a town where I knew every man, woman, and child, and where every man, woman, and child knew me, a somewhat monotonous occupation; and I fail to see anything calculated to enlarge the intellect in the acts of planting potatoes all day and eating them for breakfast, dinner, and supper. Still there is a certain amount of truth in what you say, or rather imply. The English are not an imaginative people, and they do not consider it necessary to idealize work. They labour for so much a day, and honestly say so. It is in the nature of a quick, sympathetic nation to be desultory, and the Irish are desultory till they come to England, when they suddenly develope the most marvellous perseverance, and trot up and down ladders with hods on their shoulders in a manner wonderful to behold."

"Dear Mrs. Hartley, how I wish I could make you like the Irish!" said Grace.

"I like you; is not that sufficient?" was the prompt reply.

"No, not half, nor quarter."

"Ah! my love, you are like those unreasonable women who expect their husbands to be fond, not merely of them but of the whole of their relations, to the sixth and seventh cousins."

It was a singular fact, and one Grace could not avoid remarking to herself, that on paper she and Mrs. Hartley had been much more confidential and friendly than they seemed ever likely to become while they remained face to

face. Doubtless this arose from the circum-
stance that in their correspondence Mrs.
Hartley still thought of Grace as the young
girl in whose fortunes she had once taken an
almost motherly interest, whilst Grace pictured
Mrs. Hartley as the kindly, middle-aged lady
who had petted and ridiculed and been fond
of her ever since she attained to the dignity of
long frocks and turned-up hair.

For Grace had never worn her hair in ring-
lets like Nettie ; not all the papers or irons on
earth could have given her hair that curl
which Kingslough so much admired in Miss
O'Hara ; and after having had her locks twisted
up into some hundreds of little twists and
screws, Grace would appear an hour after her
nurse had unfurled her curls with her hair as
straight as if no attempt had ever been made
to dress it in the approved fashion.

Thus it came to pass that as those were not
the days in which children's tresses were allowed to float in the wind, or stream down to
their waists through the valley between their
shoulders, Grace was condemned to have her

hair done up in two long plaits, which were sometimes worn as pigtails, and sometimes doubled up like curtain-holders, being tied together at the nape of the neck by ribbons brown or blue.

Considering that blue did not suit the child, and that a more hideous style of dressing the hair never prevailed, it may be suggested that Kingslough had some excuse for the opinion at which it then arrived concerning little Miss Moffat's looks.

Those days were gone, the days of plum-cake and delightful evenings, with two people for a whole party, and Grace allowed to make the tea; the days when Mrs. Hartley used to ask the girl to spend pleasant afternoons with her, and took her drives and walks, and was very good to her altogether.

Yes, they were gone, as the Grace of old was gone; the plain chrysalis who was now so pretty a creature, the little, grave, silent orphan who, wont to blush when any one spoke to her, could now speak for herself in any place and in any company, but who could

not talk confidentially to Mrs. Hartley, perhaps for the reason that Mrs. Hartley now felt
a difficulty in asking questions she once would
not have hesitated to put by letter.

There was a break, not caused by disagree-
ment, but by apparent lack of sympathy between them, which both felt painfully, which
each would have given much to bridge over.
I think this kind of reserve between staunch
friends is by no means so uncommon as many
people imagine. It is more difficult to get the
heart to break silence than the tongue, and
for this reason the most fluent talkers are
not those who speak of their tenderest
feelings.

How long this might have gone on it is
hard to conjecture, had there not one morning
arrived a letter for Miss Moffat, directed in a
man's handwriting. Mrs. Hartley noticed the
fact. It was the first communication from any
gentleman, except her lawyer, Grace had received since her arrival. Her friend knew
this, because she opened the post-bag and
dealt out its contents.

The whole day after Grace was silent and thoughtful. Mrs. Hartley noticed she looked in an abstracted manner out of the window, and that occasionally she fixed her eyes on her with a sort of questioning and anxious expression.

Towards evening Mrs. Hartley determined to break the ice. " That girl has something on her mind," she considered as she entered the drawing-room five minutes before dinner, " I must find out what it is," and she proved herself as good as her words.

They had dined, dessert was on the table, Grace was toying with some fruit on her plate, Mrs. Hartley had swallowed two of the three glasses of port her doctor assured her she ought to take with as " much regularity as if it were medicine."

At this precise stage of the proceedings she had made up her mind to speak, and with Mrs. Hartley, to make up her mind was to do.

" Grace," she began, " there is something troubling you."

"Yes, Mrs. Hartley, I have a very great trouble," answered Grace calmly.

In an access of excitement Mrs. Hartley poured out and swallowed that third glass of port.

"Let us go into the other room, where we can talk comfortably, my dear," she said, rising; and Grace, nothing loth, left her untouched fruit, walked across the hall into the snug little drawing-room she had learned to love so much, opening on one side to a conservatory, and on the other to a lawn kept smooth and soft as velvet.

After all, spite of its shrubs, its trees, its long sea frontage, and its acres of garden ground, there was room for much improvement at Bayview.

"If ever I return to Ireland," Grace had said to herself many and many a time, "I will have that grass kept like these English lawns."

And yet after all there is grass in the Emerald Isle smoother, shorter, closer, and softer than any in England. Only in that case sheep have been the mowers. I know an island in a lake where they fatten in six weeks, and where it is perhaps unnecessary to say stand the ruins of an old monastery.

CHAPTER IV.

GRACE TELLS HER STORY.

GRACE'S experiences of drawing-rooms in her own country had been considerable.

She had been acquainted from her childhood with immense apartments, commanding sea and land views. She knew the orthodox style of furniture which upholsterers sent in as a species of groundwork upon which individual fancy subsequently painted the form of its own especial idiosyncrasy. She had beheld acres of carpeting, hangings which were miracles of heaviness and expense, chairs first covered with green, or amber, or ponceau, or silver grey, to match the curtains, and then wrapped up in holland, to preserve their beauty intact, ponderous loo and sofa tables, everything as good as money could buy, and expected to last accordingly; these were some of the necessaries without which no drawing-room in a gentleman's house could be considered orthodox; but when all such things had been provided, it was admissible to add such other elegances as personal taste might suggest.

Personal taste or family circumstances produced occasionally some very curious devices in the way of ornamentation. Relics from Pompeii would be the attraction of one home; carved temples, cedar-wood boxes, daggers with richly-ornamented handles, spoke in another of some male relatives who had crossed the sea, and brought back flotsam and jetsom with him. Dogs, parrots, flowers, depicted in wool on canvas, testified in many homes to the indefatigable industry of its female occupants; in rare cases, rare because the materials were for those days costly, bead-work in unlimited quantities charmed the beholder; occasionally old china, which would now fetch fabulous prices in London, adorned the chiffoniers, whatnots, and cabinets of persons who had none too much money to spare, whilst in almost all cases where there were young ladies, or even middle-aged, the open piano, the litter of music, often a harp or a guitar, spoke of the love of that talent which is bestowed so much more freely on Irish than English women.

All these rooms, and many others besides, Grace had been free of; rooms with a certain stately dignity about them, rooms connected with which she had many a pleasant childish and girlish memory, but a drawing-room like Mrs. Hartley's was as far beyond her imagination as that other style of apartment generally and prudently unoccupied which obtains in the suburbs of London, and in the houses of all highly respectable and sober-minded middle class people throughout England generally.

Luxury in those days had not attained to the height to which it has since sprung. It has been reserved for the reign of her present

Majesty to witness a more rapid transition from comparative simplicity of living, lodging, dressing, spending, to the wildest extravagance of expenditure in all ranks, than has ever occurred before at any era, or in any nation; and for this reason the decorations and furniture which seemed perfection to Grace Moffat, would no doubt appear extremely poor and commonplace if catalogued for the benefit of the reader.

In the nature of almost every woman there is, I suspect, a latent, cat-like love of things soft, bright, cosy, and there was something in the whole aspect of Mrs. Hartley's drawing-room which appealed to this sense in Grace's nature. She liked walking over the thick carpet; the white sheepskin hearthrug on which generally reposed a King Charles that hated Grace with a detestation she cordially reciprocated; the fire-light reflected from mirrors, sparkling against lustres; the lovely water-colour drawings hanging on the walls; the delightful easy chairs; the statuettes; the flowers piled up in banks between the long French windows, and the conservatory filled with rare and beautiful plants; all these things were pleasant as they were novel to the rich widow's visitor.

In Mrs. Hartley's opinion, however, the very greatest ornament her room had ever held was Grace Moffat, and the admiration she always entertained for her guest was heightened as they entered the apartment together, by the new interest now attaching to her, as the older lady felt satisfied must be the case. Some misplaced affection, some love entanglement which she had kept secret until she could endure to keep silent no longer.

"Now sit down, dear, and tell me all about it; you prefer the low chair, I know," began Mrs. Hartley; but Grace answered,—

"I should like to sit on the rug close by you, if I may, and if Jet does not object to my company."

"He shall be taken away," said Jet's mistress, laying her hands on the bell.

"No!" interposed Grace. "I will try

to be amiable to him, if he will be tolerant of me," and she sat down; a pretty picture in the firelight, her black dress disposing itself in graceful folds over the white rug, her hands crossed idly in her lap, and her face upturned to Mrs. Hartley, who, stooping, kissed it almost involuntarily.

"Now who is he?" asked the widow.

"There is no 'he' in my story," Grace answered; "at least no 'he' in your sense. I hope you will not be disappointed when I tell you my trouble has nothing to do with love, but a very great deal to do with money."

"So far, my dear, I think money has been a trouble to you; when you are as old as I am you will understand the trouble of having money is by no means comparable to the trouble of being without it."

"In this case my money has nothing to do with the story."

"Then, for mercy's sake, child, tell me what has to do with it."

"I have," Grace answered; "a secret has

been confided to me that I do not know how to deal with; a responsibility has been put upon me which makes me wretched. I fully intended when I first came here to tell you all about the matter, but—"

"But what?" asked Mrs. Hartley softly; "this is the light, and you are in the mood for confession, let us get that little 'but' out of the way now—for ever."

"I will try," said Grace boldly. "You are not really changed in the least; you are the same true, dear friend you were in the old Kingslough days when Nettie made such a mess of her life; but everything about you is changed. The grandeur—don't laugh at me— and the formality, and the stateliness of your surroundings threw me back at first, and then I fancy you thought I was changed, and so—"

"Yes; you need not try to finish; spite of your occasional little whiffs of temper, you have changed, or rather developed, into one of the sweetest and most lovable women I have ever known. And now you are getting accus-

tomed to what you call my grandeur, and En-
lish ways do not seem so objectionable as they
did at first, and we are going this evening to
break the ice once and for always; and you
have a story to tell, and I am in one of my
best moods for listening."

" My story is a very short one, but it will
interest you, for it concerns the Rileys."

" Which of them ?"

" All ; father, mother, sisters, brother," answered Grace. "The night my father was
taken ill I was told something which may
affect them all most seriously. It was my intention to consult him in the matter, but after
—after his death you may imagine I forgot for
a time in my own grief the possible griefs of
other people. Before I left Ireland, however,
I received a note containing the words, ' Have
you forgotten what I told you ? ' To-day a
second note is forwarded to me repeating the
same inquiry."

" May I ask the name of the writer ? "

" No ; there is my difficulty. I am bound
to silence as regards my informant. But for

that, I should have sent for General Riley and told him all I had learned."

" The Rileys and you have not been very intimate since you were sweet seventeen ? " said Mrs. Hartley interrogatively.

" No," was the reply. " We of course are friendly if we happen to meet, but Mrs. Riley's disappointment at my refusing John was so great that she ceased visiting Bayview entirely. I felt rather hurt that she never called upon me after my loss. The General was ill; indeed his health has been bad for a long time past, but I thought and think she and the girls might have let bygones be bygones, and come and said, ' We are sorry for your trouble.' "

" It certainly would have been more graceful," remarked Mrs. Hartley ; " but, then, one never associates the ideas of grace and Mrs. Riley together. But to come to your story."

" You know there is a mortgage on Woodbrook ? "

" I knew there was one, and to know that, is to conclude there is one still. I never heard of a mortgage being paid off in Ireland; such a thing might have happened, but I do not think it likely."

"The Woodbrook mortgage has not been paid at all events," replied Grace; "but, so far as I can gather, it has changed hands."

"In whose hand is it now, then?"

"In Mr. Brady's."

"What! the man Nettie ran away with?"

"The same."

"Where on earth did he get enough money to enable him to advance such a sum?"

"I have not the faintest idea."

"What could have induced him to do a thing of the kind?"

"Revenge. He means to turn the Rileys out of Woodbrook; at least so I am informed."

"Can you trust your informant?"

"Fully; there is, I think, not the slightest hope of"—Grace hesitated; she could not say, "his being mistaken," and she would not say, "her;" so she altered the form of her sentence, and finished it by adding, " there cannot be any mistake in the matter."

Mrs. Hartley lay back in her chair and thought in silence.

She was quick enough to grasp the whole meaning of Grace's communication, and she understood sufficient of legal matters to comprehend how to a certain extent the desire of Mr. Brady's heart might be compassed.

" What can be done ? " Grace asked at length.

" I do not see that either of us can do anything," was the reply. " General Riley ought to be told by some one, and the question naturally arises by whom ? Shall I write to him, if you feel any hesitation about re-opening your acquaintance with the family ? "

" I should not have any feeling of that kind to influence me in such a case as this," Grace answered ; "but if I wrote to the General, it would be certain in some way to reach Mr. Brady's ears, and if it did—"

" Supposing it did ? "

" By putting two and two together he might,

he would, suspect from whom I received my information."

" And in that event disastrous results might ensue to your nameless friend ? "

" I believe so."

" I think you had better tell me the name of your friend."

" I cannot. I promised to keep it a secret. It fills me with such dread and apprehension to fancy what might occur if Mr. Brady ever should learn who betrayed him, that I feel tempted at times to let matters take their course. Surely, the General is old enough to manage his affairs without any assistance from me ? "

" He may be old enough, but he is far from wise enough. If Mr. Brady has really laid a trap for him, he will walk into it as innocently as a child ; and then, some fine day, we shall hear they have all to leave Woodbrook; that the shock has killed the General; and that when John returns there will not be an acre of land left of his inheritance."

" I thought of writing an anonymous letter,"

said Grace innocently; "but then no one ever takes any notice of anonymous letters."

"It is well you did not carry that plan into execution," remarked Mrs. Hartley. "I must think the matter over, Grace. It has come upon me suddenly; in fact, I cannot realize such a complication. You are positive," she went on, "that you have not been deceived; that the he, she, or it who told you the story did so in perfect good faith?"

"Yes, quite positive, the risk incurred alone would satisfy me of that, even if other circumstances had failed to do so."

"Do you know it strikes me you have taken the whole affair rather coolly, young lady!" said Mrs. Hartley. "I think, even although you did refuse John Riley, *he* would not have permitted months to pass without letting *you* know your fortune was in danger, had the cases been reversed."

"I have felt something of what you express," Grace replied, "and suffered in consequence. Had John been in this country, I should have told him at once—I should have felt safe with him—but I am afraid of telling the General. I suppose I must be a great coward, but I never dreaded anything so much as having it known the information came from me. I could have trusted John's discretion, I cannot trust that of the General or Mrs. Riley or the girls."

" Still we must not let them be utterly beggared without lifting a finger to save them. Besides, your friend must wish them to know their danger, or such a communication would never have been made ; and if harm does come of Mr. Brady hearing you are acquainted with his secrets, it seems to me that you are in no way responsible for it."

" Harm must not come, Mrs. Hartley," said Grace earnestly. " If you can think of any way in which we can let the General know without his connecting either of us with the intelligence—well ; but if not, the very best thing that could be done would be for you to write to John and tell him that he must come home.

" And find Mr. Brady ' in possession ' of the

property!" finished Mrs. Hartley. "I suspect there is no time to be lost about the matter, and that, clever as we both are, we shall have to get the assistance of some man in it. Poor John! it would indeed be hard to lose both wife and lands."

"I should have thought he might have found the former without much difficulty ere this," said Grace.

"Then, my dear, you judged Mr. John Riley, as usual, unfairly," retorted Mrs. Hartley.

Her visitor laughed. "I do so like to hear you defend him. You are thoroughly in earnest on that subject."

"Earnestness is a good quality," said the widow. "It is one in which some of your suitors have been rather deficient."

"None of them, so far as their desire to get my money was concerned, I assure you," Miss Moffat answered, which might be considered as rather a neat little tit in return for Mrs. Hartley's tat.

For a long time after they had separated for

the night the latter lady lay awake, thinking over Grace's story, and wondering who could have told her. She recalled all the people she had known in Kingslough, she puzzled her head to imagine who it might be so utterly in Mr. Brady's power as to dread the weight of his vengeance. She tried to remember if Grace had let fall any word likely to give her a clue, but in vain.

"It must be that Hanlon or else Scott—I dare say it was Scott. But, then, Mr. Brady and he could not be bitterer enemies than they are; besides, the address on that letter was written by a person of education. I feel no doubt it was Mr. Hanlon," and then all at once the truth flashed upon her, and she sat up in bed, saying almost out aloud, "It was Nettie, the man's own wife." Even in the darkness Kingslough seemed to rise before her eyes. Kingslough at high noon, with the sun dancing on the sea and a group of pitying friends gathered round a feeble old woman bewailing herself for Nettie, golden-haired Nettie, who had gone out that morning all unsuspecting to meet her fate.

Next morning Mrs. Hartley appeared at breakfast, with signs of sleeplessness around her eyes, and tokens of anxiety on her face.

"I have decided on the course we must take," she said, when they were alone; "but before I speak about it, I want to tell and ask you something."

"I know now from whom you received your information; do not be frightened, for the secret is safe with me, and it is well I do know, for otherwise we might, with the best intentions, have secured a *fiasco*. What I wish to ask is this, Is he aware she is acquainted with this affair?"

"Mrs. Hartley," said Grace quietly, "I must refuse to answer any question in connection with the individual who brought this intelligence to me. I wish it never had been brought. I am the last person in the world on whom such a responsibility should have been thrown."

"I agree with you to a certain extent. I think there are many persons in the world who would have been of more use in such a crisis than yourself. The worst of young heiresses, even if they have philanthropic impulses and amiable dispositions, is that they are apt to get slightly—"

"Selfish," suggested one of the young heiresses referred to.

"No, I do not mean exactly that; in fact, I am not exactly certain that I could express what I do mean. One thing, however, I must say, making all allowance for the difficulty in which you have been placed,—I think, Miss Grace, you ought to have made some move in the matter ere this; you ought to have told me all about it before you had been twenty-four hours in the same house with me. There, I have spoken out my mind and feel better for it. Now are you going to be very angry with me?"

"No indeed," Grace answered; "I like to be scolded, it seems as though some one loved me enough to be interested in me," and she caught Mrs. Hartley's hand and held it for a second. There were unshed tears in the eyes of both. Perhaps the same thought occurred to each at the same moment. They had wealth, and position, friends, acquaintances; they possessed those things deemed valuable by most people; and yet they were lonely creatures, the one in her youth, the other in her age.

"I shall write," said Mrs. Hartley, after a pause, "to Lord Ardmorne, or rather, I shall go to see him—he is in London now; he is so courteous a nobleman, I dare say he would come to see me if I asked him."

"That would be a far better arrangement," remarked Grace. "Your servants here could attach no importance to his visit, but his servants there might."

"Nonsense!" exclaimed Mrs. Hartley, but she gave way nevertheless, and wrote a note forthwith in which she stated she desired to have Lord Ardmorne's advice and assistance, and stating she would send her carriage to meet any train by which he might appoint to travel.

By return of post came his lordship's answer. He should be only too delighted, he said, if his advice or assistance could be of any service to Mrs. Hartley, and he would leave London by such a train on such a day.

"So far well," said the widow; "now we must have a nice luncheon for the dear old man, and you must look your very best. I suppose you are not desirous of adding any other members of the nobility to your list of suitors; but as penance for your sin of omission, you ought to make yourself very charming."

"I will try," answered Grace, and she succeeded. Lord Ardmorne was delighted with her.

When, in the pretty drawing-room, Mrs. Hartley repeated all Grace had told her to him, the visitor looked exceedingly grave.

"This thing must not be," he said; "we must save the General from ruin, and keep the estate for the son—a fine, brave, honest fellow. I never did a kindness to any young man whose subsequent career satisfied me so completely. I never receive a letter from India in which his name is not mentioned, and with approval."

Grace felt her colour rise a little at this laudation of a man she had never thought clever or remarkable in any way, and she turned her head away, so that if Mrs. Hartley glanced towards her, she might build no fancy from her face.

But Mrs. Hartley did no such thing. She was much too astute a woman to let Grace imagine she was going to plead John Riley's cause again. She had made up her mind that Miss Moffat and her first lover should marry, but she did not intend to let Grace see her game, or tell her for what stakes she was playing. Mentally, she likened her own position to that of the man who, driving pigs along the road to Cork, told all the people he met that he was proceeding in a contrary direction for fear the animals might immediately turn back.

She had guessed Grace's little peculiarities with tolerable accuracy, and she was determined not to risk damaging her favourite's chance by running counter to them.

From the tone of his letters, she knew no woman had as yet filled up Grace's place in John's heart.

" I wonder if he would still love her if they met. She is beautiful now, which she certainly was not then; but she is not quite the Grace he knew—"

Was she not? Before another twelvemonth had passed, Mrs. Hartley knew of what stuff Grace was made.

"I shall at once write to Mr. Riley, and tell him his presence is urgently required in Ireland."

"But what a pity it seems to do so, when he is getting on so well in India !"

"If he finds affairs in Ireland are able to go on without him, he can return to India; I will arrange all that."

"But it would be dangerous to wait for his return before making any move in the matter," suggested Mrs. Hartley.

"I shall not wait for anything or person," was the reply; "I shall ascertain if the statement be true—no reflection intended, Miss Moffat, on your sagacity; this can be done through the General's lawyers."

"And then?" suggested Mrs. Hartley.

"Then I shall begin to be perplexed. I do not suppose, if the interest were regularly settled, there would be any necessity to pay off the mortgage, but still I think it will have to be paid off, and if so, where is the money to come from? It is not given to every one to command capital as Mr. Brady seems able to do. I have been buying an estate lately in one of the midland counties, and it has made me very short—very short indeed. But bless me! to think of Brady aspiring to Woodbrook! No matter at what sacrifice, that must be prevented. A place I would gladly own myself."

"All my money is invested," said Mrs. Hartley. "I am afraid I could not realize any considerable sum for a long time."

"I have not the slightest idea where my money is," added Miss Moffat; "but if any of it is available, I should like to help."

"Not to be thought of," suggested Mrs. Hartley. "I am sure Lord Ardmorne agrees with me, when I say the idea ought not to be entertained for a moment."

"I really am at a loss—" began the nobleman.

" If you are sensitive, Grace, you can leave us," said Mrs. Hartley ; " if not, you can hear what I say. There was a time, my lord, when this young lady's fortune would have infused new blood into the Woodbrook estate, when a very honourable and honest young gentleman who was very fond of her asked her to be his wife. But she could not fancy him. It was a pity, still such things will happen. Without further explanation, you will see at once that if Miss Moffat stepped forward at this juncture to offer assistance, her feelings and motives might be misconstrued. Her views have undergone no change, but it might be imagined they had."

Grace sat chafing in her place, whilst Mrs. Hartley delivered herself of this long sentence, but she did not speak. Lord Ardmorne, after studying the pattern of the carpet for a moment or two, looked up and said with a twinkle in his kindly eyes,—

" Yes, I agree with you, though it does seem hard a young lady should be unable to help a friend because his son was once her suitor. These difficulties are boulders in the path of life, but still we must all face them. If, however, I am not greatly mistaken in Miss Moffat, she is one of those who are given—

> " To do good by stealth,
> And blush to find it fame,"

and, supposing money be urgently needed, I fancy she would lend it to me and let me take the credit of helping the General and his family at this crisis. You would trust me, Miss Moffat, to take as much care of your pride as I should of your fortune?"

Said Grace—"My lord, I would trust you with my life," and passed out into the conservatory, thinking that if the Glendares had been made of such stuff as this, it would have seemed a glorious lot to link her fortune with that of Robert Somerford—even although the ways and doings of the nobility are not as the ways and doings of the class from which she sprung.

" A most charming girl ! " exclaimed Lord Ardmorne, "and the case was, as you implied, serious ! "

"Yes; John Riley loved Grace Moffat, as a girl is only liked once in her lifetime. That was why he went abroad, that is why he stays abroad, that is probably the reason why he will remain single till he is middle-aged and rich. You have seen the young lady who is ' the woman ' of that man's life."

" I fancy your story ought to end, however, Mrs. Hartley, with—they lived happy ever after."

But Mrs. Hartley shook her head. Not even to this new ally did she intend to show her hand.

CHAPTER V.

ALMOST TOO LATE.

LORD ARDMORNE was as good as his word, and
better; thereby demonstrating the truth of
the frequent assertion, that those who promise little often perform much; while those
who promise much usually fail altogether in
performing.

Not in the least like the Somerfords was the
Marquis of Ardmorne. He was not handsome in person or gracious in manner, or fluent
of speech, but he was true; true in his prejudices, which were many; in his political
faith, which was becoming obnoxious even in
England; in his religion, that generally con-

demned all men—but was so in the habit of excepting special persons and cases that the damnatory clauses were practically rendered innocuous.

From what stock shall we say such a man sprang. He was not Scotch, or Irish, or English; but he was something which we are accustomed—though as I think, erroneously—to regard as a mixture of all three. He was what the tenants called a hard landlord, and yet his rents were lower than those of the Glendares.

Politically, the Glendares were on the right side to please the people. He was on the wrong; and the "hard bit," as the tenantry called it, about Lord Ardmorne was that when a man took a farm from him he had the choice of voting as his landlord wished, of thinking as his landlord thought, or of having worldly matters made uncomfortable for him.

To ensure so desirable a state of affairs, Lord Ardmorne granted no fresh leases; but let his lands at a proportionately low rental, so as to

be able to rid his farms of recalcitrant tenants
as rapidly as might be.

I do not defend the system. Of course
amongst a people so highly enlightened as our
own—in a state of society which produces
such profound thinkers, and renders the views
of even the lowest so clear and so just, as that
which recommends itself at present—it is most
desirable the freedom of action and of conscience should obtain, even if such freedom of
action and of conscience produce similar results to those England and Ireland have
both had to deplore during the last few years ;
but still those who took Lord Ardmorne's
farms did so with a perfect knowledge of consequences.

There was no secrecy about the matter. My
lord having a certain set of opinions, expected
his tenants to acquiesce in those opinions; and
they were aware of the fact.

When by reason of death—the resignation
of a member, or other causes—an election took
place, Lord Ardmorne· expected his men to
vote for his man. If they refused to do so,

my lord turned them out. They rented his
land, knowing well the full consequences of
contumacy, and if they liked to risk those consequences, it was scarcely fair to grumble (as
they did) when the marquis enforced his share
of the bargain.

If an Irish farmer of that period could only
live a struggling trader for a year in the city
of London, in this, he might well pray heaven
to deliver him from the men of our time,
and to restore him even a hard landlord like
the marquis, who expected his tenantry to
think as he thought for the sake of an exceptionally low rental and various other in-
dulgences beside.

The Marquis of Ardmorne would have found
scant favour at the hands of those gentlemen
of the press who, in the present day, are good
enough to instruct the nobility in their duties
as landlords and landowners. He was in no
way romantic. He might have forgiven a
tenant a year's rent, but he could not over-
look his venturing to have an opinion of his
own.

His manners were not genial; he could not, to reproduce an old Irish phrase, have " charmed a bird off the bush," even if he had tried to do so. He was one of those who, it is sometimes stated, strive to stop progress. His own party honestly thought they were only the breakwaters that tended to keep the perilous waves of innovation from sweeping over and destroying the land.

The Reform Bill he believed to have been the ruin of the country. Had he lived to see the Irish Church Bill passed, he would have covered his face and turned him to the wall, feeling death had lingered too long. Tenant right stank in his nostrils. Liberty of conscience was a phrase which sounded in his ears like the claptrap expression of a party who were trying to lead the lower orders astray.

The peasantry he regarded as children who, not knowing what was best for them, ought to do as they were told. There could be no mistake as to what Lord Ardmorne considered the first duty of a tenant-farmer; and if the tenant-farmer chanced to entertain a different opinion, why so much the worse for him.

On the other hand, the Ardmorne tenantry enjoyed advantages unknown to those who rented the Somerford lands. The marquis, it is true, did little or nothing in the way of improvements ; but he did not prevent the farmers improving their holdings if they pleased to do so. Lime and stone were supplied to them at almost nominal prices. The shore rights, such as the Glendares had let and the lessee sublet again, were practically free to those who, behaving themselves properly, were suffered to cultivate his lordship's lands and pay rent to his lordship's agent ; and when crops failed or sickness laid low, and the gale days came round, time would often be given to make up that rent for which, as on the Glendare estates, the farmers and their wives, and their sons and daughters, and men-servants and maid-servants, worked from morning till night from week's beginning to week's end, from the time they were big enough to pick up stones and herd cows till they were carried to their graves.

Nevertheless, the marquis was not liked
as Th' Airl had been. Though his religious
opinions were identical with their own;
though he reverenced the glorious, pious, and
immortal memory of King William; though
he had nothing but contempt and hatred for
that of James; though he was an Orangeman,
and thought "Protestant Boys" the most
charming melody ever composed; though his
watchword, like theirs, was "No Surrender;"
though his feelings towards the Pope were
identical with their own sentiments, despite
the fact that he uttered his commination ser-
vices in Parliament in more orthodox and
gentlemanly fashion than they shouted out
theirs in the streets and highways,—still, his
lordship failed to win the hearts of his
people.

He had always been a grave quiet man,
with stern features and reserved habits; a
man with a story in his life which had perhaps
made the fulfilment of his age different from
the promise of his youth; a man of strong
purposes and deep feelings; a man to like

few, but to like those few much; a man who
would have thought himself no better than a
thief, if he had left impoverished acres and a
diminished rent-roll to the next heir, albeit
that heir was neither son nor nephew, nor
aught but a distant relative who held a high
position in India.

It was to this relative he had sent out John
Riley, and the young man might pecuniarily
have done well for himself in his new appoint-
ment, had he not commenced sending home all
he could spare in order to enable his family to
live more comfortably.

He would have done them a greater kindness had he kept his money. To persons who
have always been short, the command of a little
money is a great snare as well as to those who
have never had much experience in spending;
so at least it proved with Mrs. Riley.

She had been compelled to do without so
many things during the previous part of her
life, that now when a few of them were within
her reach she tried to compass all; and the
result proved that not only was the Indian

allowance spent, but the interest on the mortgage fell into arrear.

"When the girls are married, we can soon retrench," Mrs. Riley observed, but the girls failed to marry. If they had not done so when they lived quietly and dressed plainly, and engaged themselves in those various works of a domestic kind which recommend young ladies to men of a prudent and economical turn of mind, they were certainly likely to remain unwedded when, arrayed in gorgeous attire they were met at parties and balls in Dublin, where it was their new custom to winter.

They never lacked partners, and they never were destitute of attendant swains, who found Woodbrook a pleasant sort of house at which to stay for a week or two in the summer and autumn; but although the hopes of Mrs. Riley were often excited, they always ended in disappointment. Visitors they had in abundance, but suitors none; till at length Lucy captivated a curate, whose addition to the finances of the family proved seventy pounds a year from his rector, twenty-five pounds a year from private sources, and a baronet uncle.

"Who will be certain to present him with a good living," said Mrs. Riley; though on what foundation she erected this pleasing super-structure was an inscrutable mystery to all her friends.

Things were in this state when Lord Ardmorne through his solicitors ascertained, first, that if Mr. Brady did not actually hold the mortgage he was intimately and pecuniarily associated with those who did, and that it was in his power to pull the strings which prompted the movements of the ostensible actors; second, that the interest was running back; third, that the mortgage-deed contained some unusual and stringent covenants; fourth, that the Wood-brook estates were not returning the amount of money they had once done; and fifth, that owing to failing health, the pressure of anxiety, and the more exciting life he had in the interests of his daughters been leading, the General was becoming daily less and less competent to act as his own agent and to manage his own affairs.

Altogether the family prospects were in as

deplorable a state as family prospects could be, when Lord Ardmorne's solicitor went to confer with General Riley's legal adviser and General Riley himself.

It was from the latter gentleman that information of the interest having fallen behind was elicited.

Not being pressed for it, he, as frequently happens in such cases, had not mentioned the matter to those who would have advised him to make any sacrifice in order to keep so important an affair within manageable limits.

Piteously he confessed his error, and asked, as people are in the habit of asking when counsel is almost useless, what he was to do.

It had been agreed between Lord Ardmorne and the lawyers that, in consideration of his broken health and other causes, the fact of Mr. Brady having managed to thrust his fingers into the Riley pie should not be mentioned to the General; that if a settlement of the matter could be left until the son's return, all explanations should be deferred till he came back.

The first thing to be done was clearly to wipe off the arrears of interest; but as not an acre of the Woodbrook estate was free, General Riley's solicitors said openly that they failed to see where the money was to come from.

Lord Ardmorne, however, having taken up the affair, was not going to let this difficulty stop him on the very threshold of his undertaking, and instructed his lawyer to find the amount necessary.

He did not intend to be harsh to the General, but he did tell the old man some very plain truths concerning the risk he had run of jeopardizing his son's inheritance; and he made a point of seeing Mrs. Riley, then in Dublin, and explaining to her that the old life of paring and pinching would have to be resumed if she did not wish Woodbrook to pass into the hands of strangers.

"It is all that girl's doing," groaned the poor murmuring lady. "But for her we should have been comfortable and happy years and years ago."

Which remark set the marquis thinking.

John was a fine fellow, and, spite his encumbered acres, not an ineligible *parti* even for Grace Moffat; but he failed to see how the little romance he had planned could be carried out if Mrs. Riley were to be one of the *dramatis personæ.*

The lapse of years had not improved the General's wife. Lord Ardmorne could imagine many more desirable things than a close relationship with her, and he left the house thinking matters were complicating a little, and that perhaps he should not be justified in dragging Miss Moffat into the Riley entanglement.

"Perhaps the very best thing the young man could do would be to persuade his father to sell the estate right out and go back to India. That, however, will be a matter for future discussion and consideration. Meantime, we can do nothing but clear off the arrears of interest."

In this, however, his lordship proved to be mistaken. No sooner was the interest settled than notice was served requiring the repayment of the principal at the extremely short date mentioned in the deed.

Like most of his countrymen, Lord Ardmorne had a passion for acquiring land. A townland for sale, an estate in the market, these things affected him as the news that a rare picture is to be brought to the hammer affects a collector, and Woodbrook was a property he would have felt by no means loth to add to those he already possessed.

But the knowledge of this desire tied his tongue. In the General's extremity he could not advise him to let the encumbered acres be purchased by some one willing and able to give enough for them to clear off the mortgage and leave a margin beside.

Had he stepped in at this point and counselled the General to do that which really seemed the only rational way of solving the difficulty, he would not have cared to meet the man for whose return he had written.

"I fancy it will have to come to that in the end," he said to his solicitor in reply to a remark from that gentleman, that the sooner Woodbrook passed into other hands the better it would be for every one, the General

included, " but we must leave it for the son to
decide."

" I do not exactly see how the decision is to
be left for so long a time," remarked the
lawyer. " There can be no question it is all
a planned affair, and how any man's adviser
could permit such a deed to be signed baffles
my comprehension."

" Well, you must remember when a state of
mortgage becomes chronic," said the marquis,
" people are apt to overlook symptoms that
would strike a person to whom the disease is
new. Besides which there was no choice as I
imagine in the matter. An old mortgage had
to be paid off, and under such circumstances it
is not always easy for a man to dictate his own
terms."

To which words of wisdom, coming from
a nobleman, the lawyer listened with deference
and attention as in duty bound ; but he
held naturally to his own opinion nevertheless.

· Here, then, the Rileys had arrived at a
point where two roads met, and written on the

finger-post in letters plain enough to those who could read were the words—To Ruin.

Where the other road led was not so clearly indicated. It puzzled Lord Ardmorne himself, though both long and clear-headed, to imagine what the end of it all would be. He could turn them out of the direct route to beggary, and he meant to do so, but whether the second path might not merely prove a round-about-way to the same end he was not prepared to assert.

After all there is nothing on earth so difficult as to manage another man's affairs for him, even if he be willing to let his neighbour attempt the almost impossible feat.

But about the end, Lord Ardmorne did not mean to trouble himself till John Riley's return. When that event happened, he proposed to lay the whole difficulty of the position before the younger man, and warn him against attempting to drag an endless chain of debt through yet another generation. Meantime arrangements must be made for paying off the existing mortgage; and when he had done all he could in the matter—and with a solvent nobleman and in Ireland that all was considerable,—Lord Ardmorne found a pecuniary deficiency still existed that, although not large in itself, was still sufficiently great to cause perplexity and difficulty.

Up to this point he had decided not to permit Grace to moil or meddle in the matter, now he decided to leave her to say whether she would help or not.

"I will take care she is no loser," he said to himself, "and also that she does not appear in the transaction. I certainly will buy the place if the father and son agree to sell; if not I must arrange differently, that is all. So now to see Miss Moffat, and ascertain whether she is still willing to assist in saving an old family from utter worldly ruin."

Very straightforwardly he put the state of the case before "the woman of John Riley's life," told her what he had done, and the precise way in which she could best help, that help being kept a secret between herself, himself, and

Mrs. Hartley; and if the subsequent conversation were rendered less connected by
reason of the widow's comments on the folly
of Mrs. Riley and the childish weakness of her
husband, her remarks tended at least to make
it more exciting.

"I should like to be of use to the General
or his son," Grace said with a frankness which
caused Mrs. Hartley to shake for the ultimate
success of her project; " indeed, I should like
to serve any of them. It would be a sad thing
if for lack of a friendly hand Mrs. Riley and
the girls had to leave Woodbrook."

" It is clearly Lord Ardmorne's opinion that
the sooner they leave Woodbrook the better
for all concerned," observed Mrs. Hartley.
"And in that opinion I entirely agree. If all
the poor Irish gentry were compelled to sell
their estates, and let people who have money
and sense purchase them, it would be a grand
thing for the country."

" English people seem to think there is
a necessary connection between money and
sense. I must say I fail to see the link myself," answered Grace.   I 2

"I am inclined, however, to think the English capacity to make and to keep money implies a considerable amount of sense," interposed Lord Ardmorne.

"It is not a pleasant sort of sense," persisted Grace.

"Perhaps not, but it is useful, my dear," said Mrs. Hartley. "For instance, had your grandfather squandered the fortune he made instead of leaving it to you, he might have been a more popular old gentleman, but he could scarcely have proved himself so admirable a person in his domestic relations as was the case."

"I sometimes wish he had never left me a penny," remarked Grace a little bitterly.

"What a shame for you to make such a remark, Miss Moffat, at a time when your fortune enables you to step forward to the rescue of your old friends," exclaimed Lord Ardmorne, with an affectation of playful raillery which sat upon him about as gracefully as a cap and bells might have done.

"Yes, it is a shame," Grace answered

quietly; "for about the first time in my life I feel really thankful now that I am as rich as I am."

"Many other opportunities for thankfulness from the same cause will present themselves in the years to come, believe me," said their visitor.

"I only hope they may not have to leave Woodbrook," exclaimed Miss Moffat, a little irrelevantly to the conversation as it seemed.

"Then you ought not to hope anything of the kind," rebuked Mrs. Hartley. "You should hope that John may have enough resolution and sufficient sense to free himself and his family from the incubus of debt, that must have made existence a daily and hourly torture and humiliation to the whole of them. As I said before, if a law were passed compelling the owners of heavily mortgaged properties to sell them, there might be a chance of Ireland's regeneration. As matters stand there is none."

If with prophetic eye Mrs. Hartley had been able to look forward a very little way, how she

would have longed for the Encumbered Estates
Court, and welcomed the changes every one
predicted must be wrought by it.

In those days capital and civilization were
the favourite panaceas the English proposed
for all Irish troubles. In these the same
remedies are indirectly suggested, but the
English are now quite content to leave their
sister to find both for herself.

And no doubt the present course is the
correct one. The curse of all former adminis-
trations has been that instead of leaving
Ireland's diseases to be cured by time and
nature, each fresh political doctor has thought
it necessary to try his own new course of
treatment on the patient.

Fortunately the latest and rashest surgeon
who has experimented on her so far as to cut
away the grievance most bitterly complained
of, has discovered there may be a tendency to
hysteria in the constitution of a nation as well
as of a woman, and that it does not follow
because a cry is raised, "The pain is here,"
that the arm or leg is to be hacked off with

impunity. One man has deprived Ireland of that which kings, nor queens, nor parliament, nor statesman, can ever restore to her again. Nevertheless, he may have done both England and Ireland good service, for it will be some time before the former is tempted to try the result of another such surgical operation, let the latter cry for knife and caustic as loud and as long as she will.

CHAPTER VI.

MR. BRADY'S EX-PROJECTS.

WHEN Mr. Brady found the Rileys had by accident or design checkmated him, he was, as a young clerk who chanced to be favoured with many of his inquiries about that period, remarked, "Neither to hold nor to bind."

To ruin the Rileys, to oust the proud beggars—so he styled them—out of Woodbrook, to bring the old man to his level, and to humble the pride of "that fellow out in India," had been the dearest desires of his heart for years previously.

In order to compass them he had not spared his time or his trouble; he had not objected to wade through very dirty water, he had not grumbled when asked to eat humble pie in quantity; he had not bemoaned himself when compelled to cringe to people he longed to kick, or be civil to those he hated; and now in a moment all he had saved, toiled, lived for was snatched from his grasp.

When a man first conceives the plot of either a good or a bad project it is, comparatively speaking, a small matter to find another has forestalled him in its execution. Let him, however, have nursed, tended, perfected the scheme, lain with it in his bosom at night, and taken it for his companion by day, he finds it a cruel hardship to have the one thing he fancied his own, the one good he asked in life, claimed by another.

If the punishment of deliberate wrong-doing ever could enlist our sympathies on behalf of the wrong-doer, I think it might be in a case like this, when a man having spent his all to compass his object finds at the last that it eludes his grasp; when having staked every-thing he possesses on the success of some

villanous trick in the game of life, his
intended victim, at a moment least expected,
says " Checkmate " and leaves him to curse
the board whereon his best designs, his longest-
matured schemes, have been defeated.

On Mr. Brady the news of his enemy being
at the last moment delivered out of his hands,
fell with such a shock that at first he could
not realize the depth of his own disappointment. Although the interest being paid might
have prepared him for the settlement of the
principal, he refused to believe his lawyers
when they told him the whole amount had by
some means been raised.

To incredulity succeeded all the fury of a
balked revenge, and in his rage he accused
both solicitors and capitalist with having con-
spired in General Riley's favour against himself. He declared it was through them the
owner of Woodbrook had heard of his own
interest in the matter, to which the former
replied by ordering him out of their office, and
the latter remarked that if Mr. Brady did not
put some restraint upon his tongue all trans-
actions must end between them.

"I am willing to make some allowance for you," he went on, "as I dare say the matter is as great a blow to you as it has proved a surprise to me; but I will not have such language as you used just now addressed to me by any man living; so you can take your choice, either try to be civil, or else I will have done with you and your affairs at once and for ever."

Whereupon Mr. Brady muttered something intended for an apology, adding in a louder tone,—

"If I only knew who has been meddling in my affairs I would make it pleasant. He would think twice before thrusting himself into other people's business, I can tell him!"

"Well, when you find out who it is that has upset your plans, you can tell him what you like so far as I am concerned; but, meantime, I will not have you vent your temper on me. Remember that for the future, sir, if you please."

Whether it pleased him or not, Mr. Brady knew he must remember the hint, and act upon it ; and, therefore, set his face homeward full of anger and mortification.

This was the first severe check his plans had ever received, and in proportion to the magnitude of the venture appeared the shock of his failure.

Independent altogether of his desire to beggar and humble a family he hated, Mr. Brady had looked upon Woodbrook as the El Dorado whence he should in the future dig fortune and position.   He and his friend (who, so far as disposition and character were concerned, might be considered a not unworthy match-horse even to Mr. Brady), had long previously laid their plans, not merely for the acquisition of Woodbrook, but also how they intended to make that acquisition valuable to them.

It had been proposed by Mr. Brady's coadjutor to give that gentleman a share of the profits in consideration of his fertile brain having devised the scheme, and of his unwearying industry being necessary to carry it to success.

Mr. Brady's idea, on the other hand, was by degrees to work the capitalist out. He had not decided how the feat was to be performed, but he was well aware that it would be an extremely good thing for him if he could manage to get the whole power into his own hands.

In the first instance he would require assistance, and that to a large extent, but he did not despair of finding himself ultimately the owner of, at all events, a large portion of the property.

Money and revenge—these two desirable things he hoped to compass at a single blow—and now the castle of his dreams, the fairy palace which he had mentally erected from foundation to lofty pinnacle, was level with the dust.

He had been beaten and by the Rileys. Whoever else might realize the project he had been perfecting for years, Mr. Daniel Brady should reap no advantage from it.

About the time when he first began to think of annexing Woodbrook, "going to the salt water for the benefit of sea bathing" was becoming a recognized necessity even amongst those who had never previously thought of permitting their families such an indulgence.

From inland rural districts, as well as from the towns great and small, people came trooping for that "month at the shore," which it was believed made weakly children strong, and kept healthy children strong and robust.

Each summer Kingslough was crowded by visitors. Poor cottages—no matter how small or poor, provided they were situated close on the bay—were eagerly taken by those to whom economy was an object; and it must have been plain even to a much less intelligent gentleman than Mr. Brady that, if the accommodation in Kingslough and its neighbourhood had been twice as great, willing guests might still be found to avail themselves of it.

So far, however, no one had thought of building houses solely and simply for the benefit of season residents, and it was by a plan of this kind Mr. Brady hoped to make Woodbrook pay.

Part of the property stretched down to the

sea. The water at that distance from Kingslough was represented better for bathing than that which washed the grey shore below Ballylough Abbey. The beach was of finer sand, a headland stretched out into the sea sufficiently far to suggest the idea of erecting a quay, at which steamers could anchor at almost all conditions of the tide. The scenery was wilder and more beautiful than that surrounding Kingslough. Already there was a talk of a short sea route being inaugurated not merely between Scotland and Ireland, but between England and Ireland; and Mr. Brady, though he did not erect his castle on the strength of either English or Scotch money, considered it quite on the cards that from the great manufacturing towns in Lancashire, and even from Glasgow, people might come to spend the summer at Glendare.

That was the name he proposed to confer on the new watering-place, not because he was especially fond of the Glendares, but because he considered the title one likely to recommend itself to natives and foreigners alike. He had seen enough of English people to understand

the horror which seizes them at sight or sound
of a long Irish name, such as Ballinascraw, for
instance; on the other hand, he knew the
inhabitants of the Green Isle still retained a
preference for words indigenous to the soil.

The fashion of wiping out old landmarks, by
rechristening romantic spots with prosaic
British names, had not then begun, and he
would indeed have been considered an adventurous man—adventurous to madness—who
founding a settlement on the other side of the
Channel, blew the trumpets and assembled the
people to hear the town christened Piccadilly,
Kensington, or Wandsworth, as is the case at
present.

Mr. Brady therefore decided on Glendare,
as a name likely to wear well and find favour
in the minds of the multitude. Lying idly on
his oars, looking with his bodily eyes at the
land dotted with trees, sloping so lovingly to
the beach,—his mental sight beheld villas
filling up the landscape, snug cottages
scattered along the shore, a town perhaps
climbing up the sides of the headland. The

vision grew more real every day. He had drawn his plans, he had decided from which quarry stone should be carted; he had thought how much money he could himself afford as a beginning, how much and at what rate he could raise to complete the scheme; pleasure-boats in imagination he saw drawn up on the shore, small gardens filled with flowers, lawns on which walked ladies gaily dressed,—gentlemen rich enough to pay long rents for convenient, comfortably furnished houses. There was not another property so suitable for the purpose as Woodbrook in all that part of the country; and the beauty of it was that, whilst those few acres by the sea could be so admirably utilized, the domain itself might remain almost intact, the farms still be left as they were, the former tenants still permitted to pay rents to new owners.

And all the while unconscious of the evil-eye coveting his home, his lands, his son's inheritance, General Riley pursued his way, never imagining beggary was coming to him as fast as the feet of misfortune could bring it.

Lulled into a state of fancied security—suspecting no trick, thinking of no worse trouble in the future than a day when the arrears would have to be paid—the old man was, by reason of utter ignorance, and, it may be, natural carelessness, drifting on rocks from which his ship could never have been hindered breaking to pieces,—when he was saved as by a miracle.

What would be the ultimate end it might have puzzled a wiser than the General to say, but for a time, at least, Woodbrook was though not out of debt, out of danger. Every one connected with the matter felt nothing more could be done in the affair till John came home.

Meantime it oozed out, as indeed no one strove to prevent the story doing, that Mr. Brady and his friend had laid a deliberate trap for the General, and people began to say some very hard things about the master of Maryville in consequence; all the sins of his youth and his manhood were rehearsed, as sins will be on such occasions; all the wrong he had done in his lifetime, all the right he had left undone, all his errors of omission and commission, all his subterfuges and tricks, his faults social and domestic, the grief he had caused to many an honest father and mother; these things and others like them were disinterred from the always open grave of the past, and discussed alike in mansion and cottage in the town of Kingslough, and in other towns, besides in the country districts throughout all that part.

After a fashion, he had, up to this time, been making way with his fellows. His wife was not visited by any lady higher in rank than the wife of the minister who preached at the barn-like little meeting-house a couple of miles or so from Maryville, but men of a better class, though of a bad way of living, did not object to be seen in Mr. Brady's company, and were willing to drink, smoke, make small bets and play cards with him, not merely at various hotels and inns in Kingslough and the other towns, but at his own house.

Now there came a change, nameless, per-

K 2

haps, but certain. There was no direct cut, no absolute incivility, no alteration in manner of which it was possible to take notice, but his former acquaintances were always in a hurry when he met them, always had an engagement, always had to meet some one or go somewhere, and rarely now could find time to spend an hour or two in the evening at Maryville.

After all it was not right, these men opined, to have tried to drive the old General out of Woodbrook. The line must be drawn somewhere, and Kingslough drew it at that point which Mr. Brady had tried to cross.

Kingslough considered he ought to have refrained from meddling with a gentleman. Nothing could have revealed so certainly the taint in Mr. Brady's blood as an attempt of such a nature. The marquis went up at once in public estimation. Many persons who had long been wishing to change their political creed, since Radical notions had begun to make Liberalism rather the creed of the vulgar, took that opportunity of turning their coats.

"It was a very fine thing of Ardmorne to

do," said Kingslough, Kilcurragh, Glenwellan, and the neighbouring districts. He had gone with General Riley to the Bank of Ireland himself, it was stated; he had found the extra money required beyond what the bank would advance. He had written to request Mr. John Riley's presence, and arranged that his prospects should not suffer in consequence. In a time of trouble he had proved more than a friend, and then it was so clever of him to have found out that danger menaced the Rileys, and of what nature.

Of course, some one must have given him a clue, but he followed it up to the last inch of thread. Then came the question, who could have hinted the matter to him?

Conjecture, which it is never possible to balk, guessed every likely and unlikely person in the county. Rumour, which is the readiest inventor of fiction on earth, prepared a score of circumstantial tales on the subject, and ran them through society with as much regularity as any other serial writer might.

On the whole, public opinion inclined to the

belief that Mr. Dillwyn was the person who had opened Lord Ardmorne's eyes. It was well known that when the new earl succeeded to the title, Mr. Brady had taken a journey in order to malign Mr. Dillwyn, and secure the agency for himself, and so much unpleasantness had in consequence arisen that Mr. Somerford's step-father actually did resign, offered on certain conditions to vacate Rosemont, and expressed his opinion of Mr. Brady and the Glendares in language as remarkable for its force as its plainness.

It was only at the earl's earnest entreaty he continued to act until another agent could be found.

"And that other agent will not be Mr. Daniel Brady in this earl's time," said Mr. Dillwyn triumphantly, on his return from foreign travel—which remark clearly proved that the feelings he entertained towards the owner of Maryville were not strictly Christian in their nature.

Society at Kingslough had for so long a time been accustomed to disagreements be-

tween the Glendares and their agents, that it
had paid comparatively little attention to this
last dispute, except to marvel whether Mr.
Dillwyn would really go, and if so who would
step into his shoes. But now when every one
was anxious to know who it was that enlightened Lord Ardmorne, the passage between the agent and Mr. Brady was remembered, and a certain significance attached
to it.

In a word, though rumour invented and
circulated fifty stories, this was the one to
which people, as a rule, inclined. Mr. Brady
himself was perhaps the only person who attached no importance to it. As at first, he believed that either his own or his friend's lawyer,
or his friend himself, had proved unfaithful ; so
at last he believed that one or other of the persons with whom he was most closely connected
by ties of interest had — by imprudence or
of *malice prepense*—betrayed his plans.

No one else, he was positive, had the
faintest knowledge of them. By intuition Mr.
Dillwyn could not have guessed his tactics, and

it mattered little who it was that had finally carried the news to Lord Ardmorne, when once the secret escaped from the custody of those who ought to have held it secure.

To discover the person who originally betrayed it, suddenly became the most paramount business of Mr. Brady's life, and Nettie often wondered to herself whether the best thing she could do might not be to run away to the uttermost ends of the earth, taking the children with her.

"For if he ever finds it out he certainly will kill me," thought the wretched woman, and she thenceforth lived in a constant agony of fright. After all, no matter how tired a person may be of the business of existence, one would like to have a choice as to the mode of getting rid of the toil and the sorrow; and perhaps the most repulsive way of having the trouble ended seems that of being murdered.

There had been times when Nettie felt tempted to bring matters to a conclusion for herself—and that method of shortening the weary day now seemed luxurious by comparison with any termination which involved the ceremony of *un mauvais quart d'heure*, with Mr. Brady as an essential preliminary.

So far as affairs at the Castle Farm were concerned, General Riley's business took precedence of Amos Scott's. Having quarrelled with his own solicitors, Mr. Brady had to carry the Scott difficulty elsewhere. Out, Mr. Brady was determined the farmer, his wife, and his children should go ; but short of pulling the house down about their ears, there seemed no possibility of getting rid of them ; and for all his braggart airs, he was not prepared to take a step of that kind if he could avoid doing so.

That rough-and-ready method of ejectment, which found such favour in the south and west, never recommended itself to the northern understanding. The thing has been done, of course : the roofs have been stripped off ; the windows taken out ; the doors torn from their hinges ; in extreme cases the very walls undermined, and the house razed with the ground ; but patient as the northern temperament is, I doubt if a landlord could enjoy much ease of mind supposing he saw a man like Amos Scott sitting by his naked hearth— with the heavens for his rooftree, and the wind and the rain blowing and beating on his head.

Upon the whole, supposing imagination presented the picture of such a reality, the landlord's dreams—let right be on his side or wrong—would be of coffins and of a violent exit into that other world where all the vexed questions of this will—as we fondly hope—be settled to the satisfaction of the poor, the oppressed, the broken-hearted.

Curious to say, although Mr. Brady was a bully he was not also a coward; which seems as inconsistent a statement as to say a negro is not black. Nevertheless, it is the truth. The man was not destitute of physical courage. He had writhed mentally under the taunts hurled at him by the Rileys; but he would not have feared a stand-up fight with the son —a hand to hand struggle, with liberty given to each to kill if he were able.

Nevertheless, Mr. Brady had gone almost as far with the Scotts as he cared to do. He had dug their potatoes and sold them, cut the grass and saved it, reaped the corn and carried it, sown the land with seed, that was again hastening to fruition; but beyond this he hesitated to go. The law must do the rest, he said; but spite of the fact of justice being on his side, he found the law liked the task of turning Amos Scott out on the world rather less than he did.

When a bailiff came to take possession of the household gods, gathered together carefully, anxiously, in the first part of the Scott's married life, he was received by husband and wife, one armed with a blunderbuss and the other with a pike, a relic of ninety-eight.

"Honest man," said Amos, miscalling him in an access of civility, "honest man, if ye want to sit down to rest ye're kindly welcome; if ye want bite or sup, we can give ye share of what we have ourselves, water and a meal bannock; but if ye lay a finger on anything in this house and claim for that devil Brady I'll shoot ye dead. I've made up my mind to slay the first who meddles with the inside of that half-door, so if anything happens your blood will be upon your own head, not upon mine."

The result of which speech was that the man neither stopped nor took breath till he found himself in Kingslough again. There was a steady light in Scott's eye, and a suggestiveness about the way in which he kept his finger on the trigger, ill-calculated to make visiting at the Castle Farm pleasant to a person of the bailiff's profession.

Afterwards Amos declared " He only meant to fear the man ; " but if this were so his sport was sufficiently like earnest to carry conviction with it.

Matters had arrived at this pass, in a word : people whispered Scott was dangerous and that Mr. Brady went armed. Further, popular sympathy was with Scott, and the very ballad singers had long slips of badly printed doggrel reciting the doings of Mr. Daniel Brady from his youth upwards, and enlarging upon the fact not only of his having "decoyed a lovely maiden to a land beyond the seas," but of his trying subsequently

> "To cajole a gallant gentleman,
> And leave his son so poor."

Some kind friend managed that Nettie should be favoured with a sight of one of these precious productions.

"If he kills me one day they will sing all about that through the streets," she thought with a shiver.

Blue eyes and golden hair, what a day's work you wrought when in the bright sunshine you went away with Daniel Brady, trusting the whole future of your young life in his hands.

CHAPTER VII.

KINGSLOUGH IS PLACARDED.

PUBLIC opinion is treacherous and unmanage-
able as the sea. One hour a man is sitting
high and dry watching the waves encircle
some far away object; the next he beholds
them hurrying in to engulf himself.

Once the tide sets against any person, it
increases in volume and strength every moment, but there are no precise means of knowing when it will turn in this manner or of
telling why it has done so.

Fast as they could flow the waters of
popular dissatisfaction were running against
Mr. Brady.

At a local meeting held at Glenwellan, which he had the courage or the hardihood to attend, he was hissed, whilst General Riley's appearance proved the signal for loud and prolonged applause.

Some who were sufficiently indifferent to both men to be able to observe accurately, reported that Mr. Brady turned white to the lips at a display of feeling so decided and so unexpected; and this is sufficiently probable, since those who are the most ready to defy the opinion of their fellows are the least willing to put up with the consequences such defiance usually entails.

Be this as it may, Mr. Brady a few days later was not greatly surprised when on offering to transfer his business to a more scrupulous firm of solicitors than those to whom he had previously entrusted the conduct of his difficulties, the proposal was courteously but firmly declined.

"I shall live it down," thought Mr. Brady as he strode out of the office, his hat crushed a little over his brows.

He had said the same thing before, and he had done it; but after all, each year in a man's age, each upward step he has climbed, render that "living down" a more difficult business to perform.

It is impossible to go on having a leg broken and reset without becoming slightly a cripple, and it is more impossible still that a character shall go through a blackening process time after time and come out white in the end.

Mr. Brady had set himself a harder task than he imagined when he talked of living down the effects of his latest error, and if he did not know this Nettie did; Nettie who, hearing all that was going on, having read those ballads which found swift sale at the somewhat high price of one halfpenny each, having seen the "dour" looks cast on her husband in the barn-like meeting-house, ventured to ask him if he did not think it would be better to sell all they possessed and remove to another part of the country.

Whereupon, he turned with passionate fury, with the mad anger of a brutal nature, addressing the only person who was completely hopelessly in his power, and reproached her with having been the curse of his life, the ruin of his prospects, the sole cause of every misfortune that had befallen him.

"I wish to God I had never set eyes on you," he said. "If I must be such a fool as to marry, I ought to have married some one who would have been a help instead of a burden, a woman capable of doing something besides bringing a tribe of fretful, delicate children into the world."

"You ought to have married a woman, Daniel Brady," answered Nettie calmly, "who the first blow you gave her would have had you up before the magistrate and punished for it."

"None of your insolence or it will be worse for you," he interrupted.

"Who," continued Nettie, shrinking a little with a physical terror which had become habitual, "would have insisted on having things suitable for herself and her children, and who, if you had not provided them would have left you."

"Perhaps you are thinking of doing something of the kind," he suggested with the demon which was in him looking threateningly out of his eyes.

"No," she said wearily; "I do not care about anything for myself now, it was only for the children's sake I spoke; only to get them away from a place where their father's sins are sung through the streets, where—"

He did not let her finish the sentence. He struck her down where she stood, and with a parting piece of advice to "keep a quieter tongue in her head or it would be worse for her and her brats too," left the room, banging the door after him.

There was nothing in this so particularly new as to astonish Nettie. She was not much hurt, but as she raised herself slowly to a sitting position, she put her hand to her head with a gesture as of one suffering some cruel pain.

"How long," she murmured, "how long can I bear it? God grant me strength to endure to the end. If mothers could foresee what ' Deliver us from evil' may some day come to mean, they might hope their babies would never live to learn a prayer."

Mr. Brady's mother it may reasonably be supposed had been tempted to indulge in somewhat similar thoughts before death considerately removed her from a contemplation of her son's demerits ; and certainly public opinion had so rapidly discovered all the shortcomings of the owner of Maryville that it was tacitly admitted, (so far as human judgment could understand), if he had never been born it would have been better for him and all belonging to him.

One of the effects of this widely-spread prejudice against a man who, determined to rise by his own efforts, had certainly spared no pains in the attempt, was that from having his wrongs comparatively speaking overlooked Amos Scott became at once a popular and distinguished individual. Letters were sent to certain newspapers on the subject of tenant-right, in which Scott's case was mentioned. Leaders were written referring directly to the still unsettled dispute at the Castle Farm, and indirectly to the attempt of one of the disputants to appropriate the inheritance of a gentleman of whom the county was deservedly proud.

Mr. Brady threatened to proceed against the proprietor of one of the Kilcurragh papers unless an apology were inserted, but the proprietor inserted no apology, and no proceedings were instituted. A man who has a whole county against him may well be excused for dreading the cross-examination of an Irish barrister, and this man dreaded it with a wholesome horror, and was discreet accordingly.

All this time Amos Scott was retailing his grievances to lawyer after lawyer, walking many miles to " get speech " of gentlemen he thought might take his part, and get him his rights as he called them.

He would be off early in the morning—a piece of oat-cake, or griddle bread, in the pocket of his home-spun blue frieze coat, and he would come home at night foot-sore and weary, having broken his fast with no other food save that mentioned, washed down by a draught of water from some way-side brook, too tired to eat, too sick at heart to sleep.

For all men were in the same story. Whether they expressed sorrow for his misfortunes or told him by their manner his affairs were no concern of theirs, the result proved identical. Nothing could be done in the matter. No money—no influence—no lapse of time—no amount of trouble could undo the evil brought by that promise which the Earl had forgotten almost as soon as made.

Lawyers of course took a prosaic view of the affair, and simply assured Scott there was no use in throwing good money after bad; that he had no case, and they could not make one for him; whilst even those private individuals who commiserated him most, could not refrain from expressing wonderment at the utter simplicity which caused him to take no manner of precaution for his own safety in the transaction.

"What would you have had me do, sir?" he asked one gentleman piteously. "What more did I want than Th' Airl's word? Sure, if I had told him I'd do a thing, that would have been as good as any bond, and me only a poor man labouring with my hands to keep me and my wife and the family.

"Says Th' Airl to me, says he,

"'The land's yours for three lives longer, and you can put in one of the three for yourself.'

"So then I asked him, would I take the money on to the agent, and he says,

"'No, you may give it to me.'

"And I counted the notes into his own hand. I mind how the sun shone on a ring he had on his finger while I was doing it. Then I asked him about the writings, and he said, they couldn't be signed till Henry the young airl came of age, but that if Lady Jane died before he did so, he would see me safe.

"He was riding off when he turned, and said,

"'I suppose though, my good fellow, you are on the right side, because if not, I must give you back your money, and let somebody that have the renewal.'

"He said it joking like. He was always free and pleasant in his way Th' Airl."

A simple enough narrative, which no one who heard it doubted the truth of for a moment. A narrative which was recited by many a stump orator of the day, and stirred the hearts of thousands who were or who imagined themselves to be labouring under injustice as great and as irremediable.

Simple as it was, however, no human being could persuade Amos Scott that any of his listeners perfectly understood it. Had even one amongst the number done so, he felt quite satisfied he should hear no more said about his defiance being worse than useless.

"If I could only make yer honour comprehend it," he said reproachfully, though respectfully, to Lord Ardmorne's agent, who spite of his having, as he assured Amos over and over again, nothing whatever to do with the Glendares or their tenants, had been seized upon by the farmer for help and sympathy, "you would see it as I see it."

"Mr. Scott," answered the agent solemnly,

"if I could only make you comprehend it, you would see how hopeless your position is."

When, however, did argument or assertion convince an obstinate, uneducated man. If such a miracle were ever wrought by earthly means, it was not in the case of the poor misguided farmer who wandered about the country seeking help from this one and that, discoursing about his wrongs in lonely cabins, telling his grievances to chance companions, wasting his slender means in feeing such lawyers as would take his money, and in providing food for such of his family as were still at home.

David had returned Miss Moffat's loan to that young lady with a characteristic note, in which, after thanking her for her goodness and telling her how troubled in his mind he was to hear of the master's death, he went on to say how grateful he should be in case she had no need of the money if she would lend it to his next oldest brother, who was mad to join him."
And now two of the sons were in America, two of the daughters in service, and Reuben ready

to take a schoolmaster's place when the old people could spare him.

"But I can't leave them yet, Miss Grace," he wrote. "I am not much use here, I know; but still I can speak a word to the father when he comes home at night, and the mother is too heartsore to ask him 'what luck?' She is keen on now for us to start for America, but the father won't hear talk of it. David sent her home a pound two months ago, and another last week; a man who went out from these parts twenty years since, and who has never been in Ireland again till now, brought it, and some odds and ends of presents, amongst other things a walking-stick that we often say would have just pleased the master; it is so light, though so big; it is made from the root of the vine, Mr. Moody says, and seems wonderful handy for almost any purpose. He tells us America is the poor man's country, and it seems like it. He went away with as little as any of us, and he has come home dressed like a gentleman, with gold studs in his shirt, and a gold watch and chain, and not a word of Irish in his tongue. It is just wonderful to hear how like a native-born American he talks. He tried to persuade my father to leave what he calls the 'rotten old ship' and make for 'new diggins,' but my father bid him not talk about things he has no knowledge of, and the decent man went away, offended like."

But in this Reuben Scott chanced to be mistaken; Mr. Moody did not cease visiting at the Castle Farm because he was offended with its owner. He only did so as he chanced to remark to an acquaintance, because he never had cared for society where "pistols and bowie knives were lying about, and he guessed there would be one or the other at work before Scott moved away from his clearing."

Affairs had arrived at this pass when Mr. Brady, finding the law in his own province slow to assist him, decided on going to Dublin and seeking counsel there.

Not having confined to his own bosom the purport of this journey, the Kingslough rabble got hold of it, and decided that an auspicious time for giving public expression to their feelings had arrived.

A meeting therefore was convened to take place on the day of Mr. Brady's departure, when it was decided that gentleman should be hung in effigy, and a scaffold for this laudable purpose was actually in course of erection, when an extremely strong hint from the magistrates stopped its further progress. Not to be defeated, however, within twenty-four hours Kingslough and its neighbourhood was startled from its propriety by the sight of monster bills, which occupied every available space where it was possible to placard the announcement, stating that the body of Mr. Daniel Brady would be removed from Somerford Street to its place of interment on the following day, at four o'clock P.M., when the attendance of friends would be esteemed a favour.

Now Somerford Street—not an inconsiderable thoroughfare in the early days of Ballylough—had by a not infrequent turn of times' wheel become one of the lowest, dirtiest, most disreputable lanes in Kingslough—a lane where vice and filth caroused in wretched fashion together; where sin and misery waved their rags in defiance of law and decency; whence respectability fled as from the plague; where shame, remorse, repentance, hope, could not exist for an hour, save it might be—and sometimes God be praised it was—for a few hours in the last extremity.

To condense the whole matter into a sentence, Somerford Street was as bad a street as could have been found even in the Liberties of Dublin, and its inhabitants were as little like men, women, and children, as men, women, and children can ever be. It was a place which, even in its own small way, need not have been afraid to hold up its head with very much more notorious courts and lanes London is sufficiently blessed to reckon within a certain area of Charing Cross at the present day; and it was from this den, inhabited by vice and misery, that Mr. Brady's obsequies were announced to take place.

What did it mean? Kingslough asked itself

in a dull, stupid, inconsequent sort of
way.

In a few hours more Kingslough knew, for
over the first bills were pasted a second series
so scurrilous, so profane, that nowhere out of
the Isle of Saints could so scandalous a broad-
sheet have been produced.

They were not torn down. Decent people
did not care to be mixed up in such an affair ;
the authorities were averse to acting in the
matter without advice and consultation, and
perhaps feared, as authorities in great cities
have since unwisely feared, to make mountains
out of molehills by premature interference.

So Kingslough read, and held up its hands,
or gravely shook its head, or passed on without sign, or smiled with grim approval of the
atrocious bill, or expressed its sympathy in
drunken words full of significance, and looks
more significant still.

It was the early summer time. Once again
the crops were springing and ripening at the
Castle Farm. Crops not sown this time by
Amos or one belonging to him ; and it was

light in that northern latitude so soon in the morning, that to get out in the grey dawn almost involved sitting up during the few hours of the short night.

Nevertheless, in the grey dawn some one was astir tearing down those disgraceful placards. Slowly and calmly the sea came rippling in on the shore, closely the blinds were drawn on the Parade and in the houses of Glendare Terrace, in the east there was still not a glimpse of the rising sun, whilst rapidly and nervously the flitting figure did its work.

All at once a burly brute, who, having business far away at an early hour had risen betimes, turned a corner suddenly, and caught sight of a dark figure engaged in the work of destruction. With a whoop and a shout he rushed forward; with a shriek the woman, for it was a woman, fled.

Swift as she was he gained upon her; she left the rough pavement and sped like a greyhound along the more level road, all in vain. Panting, sobbing, she heard the thud of his heavy shoes almost at her heels, felt in imagination his hand on her shoulder, when suddenly turning the corner of a street to try to escape him, she fell almost into the arms of a third person, who, in less time than it takes me to write the words, had planted a good serviceable blow between the eyes of her pursuer, and sent him sprawling in the gutter.

"Mrs. Brady," he said, turning to the apparition which had so suddenly greeted his vision, "what in Heaven's name has brought you here at this time of night?"

"I—" she began in a broken husky voice, "I heard of it all and came," at which point she gave up trying to explain, and dropped down in a heap on the nearest doorstep insensible.

"Here is a delightful complication," thought Mr. Hanlon as he looked first at the burly brute just gathering himself together, and skulking off with a look of ineffable hate overspreading his countenance, and then at Mrs. Brady, whose light figure he supported with one hand while fumbling for his latch-key with the other.

Had the gift of second sight been vouchafed to that clever surgeon and mistaken orator, he would have fled from Kingslough within an hour more swiftly than Lot did from the Cities of the Plain, to avoid being mixed up with the evil to come.

CHAPTER VIII.

BAD NEWS.

PASSING through Kingslough *en route* from India to Woodbrook, Mr. John Riley was so fortunate as to obtain a good view of the vagabond procession that accompanied Mr. Brady's effigy to its resting-place; and perhaps that gentleman had never felt so little proud of his countrymen as when—his driver compelled to draw the horse on one side and halt, in order to allow the rabble to pass—he beheld a crowd composed of the very scum of the population marching in irregular fashion to the noise made by several cows'-horns, a fife, a drum, and a fiddle, the latter musical instrument being

played by a blind man seated in a rickety
cart, to which, with sundry broken leathern
straps and stronger pieces of rope, a half-
starved donkey was harnessed.

There they came, the lowest of the low,
accompanied by women who looked as though
they had lost every attribute of their sex, and
were indeed only human because of their utter
abject misery. On they came, most of them
women, ragged, bonnetless, shoeless, and stock-
ingless, clad in dirt as in a garment; their
masses of unkempt, uncared-for hair, twisted
into loose untidy coils at the back of their
heads ; a terrible sight to one who had almost
forgotten such a sight was to be seen. Nor
were the men one whit better, shambling along
in old shoes never made for them, with torn
coats or jackets, with trousers from which
every trace of the original cloth had vanished,
with hats and caps of every conceivable form,
battered, rimless, napless, or ragged, with tufts
of hair in some instances shooting like rank grass
through holes in the crown, with faces always
wild, reckless, haggard, now lit up with an

almost demoniac excitement. On they came, cheering, cursing, singing, shouting, followed pell-mell by all the rosy-cheeked, fair-haired, bare-legged, bare-footed, dirty-faced children in the town, who danced after the procession right merrily. Some there were better clothed than those composing the mass of the crowd: men with sedate faces and unmended coats and sound shoes, who looked as though they gave their presence as a solemn duty, but who were careful to keep on the sidepaths, and allow the unwashed multitude in the roadway as wide a berth as possible.

In the middle of the people, borne on the shoulders of four stalwart ruffians, was the so-called corpse; a door torn from its hinges serving the purpose of a bier, and a piece of sacking answering for a pall.

A hideous spectacle altogether; but then as now there was no particular reason why the innocent diversions of the masses should be interfered with.

"What are they doing—what does it mean —what is it all about?" asked Mr. Riley of his driver. M 2

" Don't keep your face turned their way," answered the man in a hurried whisper. " If they even* who you are they'll be wantin' to chair you. It's burying Brady's effigy all this is about. Come, now, keep your distance all of you," he continued, addressing some irrepressible beggars, who, seeing a stranger, at once appealed to him for help, and with scant ceremony he began using his whip to right and left, and so kept the most importunate at bay till the procession had passed.

"What has Mr. Brady been doing now?" asked Mr. Riley with some curiosity, as they drove on once more.

"Nothin' much fresh, yer honour; but they've taken a hathred to him, and wanted to hang him, but the magistrates wouldn't let them put up a gallows, so now they're goin' to bury him on the sea-shore. He's away to Dublin to get all the law money can buy against Amos Scott, and that has stirred them up a bit."

Meantime the crowd surged on to the beach, which the receding tide had left bare, and

---

* Guess.

across the shore still wet and glistening, through pools of water, over slippery bunches of seaweed, the bearers went, stumbling and staggering, whilst the band playing more lugubrious airs than ever led the way, and the men and the women and the children followed hooting, laughing, screaming.

Arrived at the extremest distance from high-water mark it was possible to reach, a hole was dug and the body tossed in. The most voluble member of the assemblage then mounted the donkey-cart, and with a sheet wrapped round him to imitate a surplice, proceeded to deliver a travesty of the Burial Service over the grave. In language as deficient of ordinary decency as it was full of horrible profanity, he recounted the history of Daniel Brady from his cradle to his grave, and narrated to an admiring audience the way of life chosen by this man whose loss they had to deplore. A few there were among the bystanders possessed of courage enough to cry "Shame!" at passages more than usually ribald and impious, but their voices were drowned by shrieks of laughter, by cheers and exclamations of appreciation.

When the merriment had reached its height, however, a man came picking his steps over the shore, and making his way a little into the crowd, shouted, "Silence!" in a tone that rang high above the clamour, and seemed to wander out like the dying sound of a clarion's note over the quiet sea.

"We can't have any more of this," he said. "Robert Sweeney take off that rag and get out of the cart.   McIlwrath, I am astonished to see a respectable man like you countenancing such disgraceful proceedings. Be off home all of you. I shall not allow you to stay here another minute."

"You'll let us cover the poor fellow up snug, or the tide 'll be taking him a dance?" entreated one man with a squint and short of an arm.

"Be quick about it then," was the answer, and the sand was shovelled in, and then trodden down by heavy boots, each by-stander who wore such articles giving the grave a hearty kick, even the women left the prints of their

fect on the surface ; and then Mr. Sweeney having laconically disposed of both body and soul
in a sentence it is unnecessary to transcribe, but
which restored thorough good humour amongst
the cowed and sullen assemblage,—the people
straggled off, leaving the constabulary officer
alone.

"It was better to let them finish their
work," he said to himself as he paced slowly
by the water's edge, looking after the retreating
rabble, "or we should have had the thing
tossing in and out with every tide.   After all,
Mr. Brady," he went on, "if straws do show
how the wind blows, I should not particularly
care to stand in your shoes to-day."

Of the scene which greeted his arrival in
Kingslough, Mr. Riley wrote a vivid description
to his old friend Mrs. Hartley; nothing could
have pleased that lady better.   She felt delighted that his first letter from Woodbrook
should be one she could show Miss Moffat.

Handing it over to that young lady, she said,
" Here is an Irish sketch drawn by a native.
It is certainly not complimentary to your

favourites.   Read the letter, it will amuse you."

But as Grace read, her face betokened anything rather than amusement; and when she finished, she folded it up and remarked,—

"I think Mr. Riley's taste in writing that letter open to question."

"You should try and excuse his want of appreciation, Grace; remember he has laboured under the disadvantage of living many years in another country and amongst other people."

"It is of very little consequence whether I excuse him or not, I imagine, "replied Miss Moffat. She had not yet seen this man returned from foreign parts. Mrs. Hartley had been visited by him in London, and reported that he was much changed in every respect.

In what way this change exhibited itself, Grace did not care to inquire. That he had not come home to be at her beck and call, she perfectly understood from Mrs. Hartley's manner of saying,—

"He begged me to give his kind regards to Miss Moffat if she had not quite forgotten an old acquaintance."

From that day it was a noticeable thing, Miss Moffat never spoke of him as John.

The old familiar name, retained almost unconsciously through years, was laid aside and Mr. Riley took its place. Of course, he could know nothing of what she had done for him and his. How she had offered her money to save Woodbrook. How she had looked forward to seeing him once again with a mingled feeling of pleasure and pain, and it was right, quite right, he should look upon and think of her almost as a stranger.

" A lover never can be a friend," she thought a little bitterly. " He never is able to forget having been refused," which is not perhaps so unnatural as Grace seemed inclined to imagine.

And now came this letter; ah! the John she remembered never would have written such an one—never could, she might have conceded.

His proclivities had always of course been towards Toryism, but he was not hard against the people; he knew their faults, but he loved

their virtues; and now the first day he returned
he could write an account of what he saw,
and turn the very sins of the Irish into
ridicule.

Further, he never once mentioned Nettie,
although it was her husband's effigy he beheld
borne along by the populace, and he said
little about Woodbrook and the state in which
he found affairs; of Lucy's marriage the only
mention he made was a remark to the effect
that, following the traditions of the family,
she having no fortune had cast her lot with a
husband who had no fortune either.

Altogether Grace felt far from satisfied.
Mr. Riley recently returned from India, and
John—dear old John of the happy days at
Bayview—were two very different persons. On
the whole Miss Moffat felt grateful to Lord
Ardmorne for arranging the Woodbrook
mortgage without any great amount of help
from her.

"It might have made it very awkward,"
she considered. "He might have fancied it
necessary to be civil to me in consequence."

And this as matters 'stood, Mr. John Riley evidently did not imagine necessary.

At the end of his letter, he begged to send his kind regards to Miss Moffat. That was all. No sentence about Bayview, no reference to the places both of them knew so well. To Miss Moffat it was rather a new feeling that of being left out in the cold, and she did not like it.

Mr. Riley's letter, however, supplied her with food for reflection besides that enumerated.

Hitherto Grace had merely known vaguely that Mr. Brady was an undesirable acquaintance, a man fond of driving hard bargains, of overreaching his neighbours if he could; a man of whom his wife stood in dread, of whom the world had nothing to tell which redounded to his credit, but now all these sins and shortcomings were italicized in her mind, and a dread of some great evil befalling Nettie in consequence of the information she had given began to haunt her night and day.

She was totally in the power of this man

whom the people vilified; whose effigy they had carried through the streets, and buried with every act of contumely they could devise. She was, though in her own country, friendless, penniless, helpless.

She had dared much in order to save those who, though her own relatives, formerly discarded her; and this very courage and forgetfulness of wrongs in a great extremity helped to recommend Nettie more tenderly than ever to her old friend.

What could she do to make matters better for her? Even in the solitude of her own chamber, Grace blushed and winced to think all she could offer any one was money; but still believing the day might come when Nettie would need it, she sat down and wrote her a long touching letter, saying how hurt she felt to hear of some recent events just come to her knowledge; how she dreaded lest evil might arise out of past circumstances, to which she need not refer more particularly; how she begged and implored her if evil did arise to come at once to England and the writer. In a postscript Grace added that, lest she should at any time want money on a sudden emergency, she enclosed sufficient to meet whatever exigency might arise.

This letter she enclosed in one to Mr. Hanlon, begging him to give it into the hands of the person to whom it was addressed.

As she did so, Grace could not help smiling, and yet sighing at the memory of her Pharisaism when first Nettie devised this mode of communication.

"Ah! I did not know so much then as I do now," thought Miss Moffat, speaking mentally, as is the habit of young ladies of small experience and limited worldly knowledge, as if she were about seventy years of age.

To this letter, after some delay, came an answer.

Nettie returned the money. She dared not keep it, she said, or she would have done so. She should never have a moment's peace were it in the house, lest it might be discovered. Earnestly, though in few words, she thanked Grace for all her kindness; but "do not

write to me again," she added, " it is too great
a risk to run. If ever you are able to help
me, I will let you know. I never can doubt
you or forget the pleasant days that may
come again no more for ever. If I never see
you in this world again, remember Gracie I
love you far, far, more at last than I did at the
first. I did not think I could cry, no matter
what came or went ; and yet still as I write
good-bye, the words are blotted with tears."

The days went on, and Mrs. Hartley and
Grace were planning an autumn tour, with a
half-formed intention of lengthening their
foreign travel by going on to Rome and
wintering in the Eternal City.

To Grace the idea was very pleasant. To
Mrs. Hartley the prospect, much as she valued
English luxuries and prized home comforts,
not disagreeable.

" I should not go unless you were with me,"
she said, however, to her visitor ; and Grace
pressed her hand in reply.

The two women were exactly suited to each
other. Mrs. Hartley's unvarying cheerfulness ;

her sound common sense ; her abundant
worldly knowledge; her stores of information;—
these things were very good for a young
woman like Grace, who was naturally somewhat dreamy and imaginative, and whose
experiences of society, of men and women, and
manners and morals, were, notwithstanding her
feeling that she had been living and learning
through centuries, had hitherto been limited
to an extremely small circle.

On the other hand, Grace was the very
person with whom to live happily. There were
no wills and musts in her nature ; she had no
ways of her own that she insisted upon other
people travelling ; she was amiable, generous,
frank, and gentle-mannered, and, to crown all
her other excellences, she was, as Mrs. Hartley
said, as good as a picture to look at.

To women whose day, if they ever had one,
is over, who have ceased to compete for those
prizes of love and admiration which all women
are anxious to secure, even though they may
not put themselves forward in the struggle,
there is something extremely pleasant in the

contemplation of a pretty face, and Grace's face was grateful to Mrs. Hartley's critical eyes.

"I wonder what John would think of her now," she often asked herself. "Would he fear to make a second attempt to win her, or dare I hope all may come right in the end. She is the wife for him, he is the husband for her, if they both can only be induced to think so. I must contrive to get him to join us somehow abroad," which was indeed the secret reason for Mrs. Hartley's advocacy of the foreign tour and her hesitation on the subject of Rome.

"Rome is a long way off," she argued, "but we shall see what we shall see ; time enough to settle about where we shall winter when the autumn comes."

Things as regards Grace were in this tranquil state, when one afternoon, while Mrs. Hartley was out on a visiting expedition, from which her guest had begged to be excused, Miss Moffat, seated in a low chair by the window of her own especial sanctum, a small morning room which had been fitted up for and appropriated to her use, took the ' Times ' that chanced to be lying close to her hand.

It was a warm day, one of those glorious summer afternoons so frequent in England, which are trying nevertheless to those born and bred in a colder climate, and Grace, tired and languid, let her eyes wander over the sheet, reading nothing in particular, but culling a paragraph here and another there with a sort of lazy and unexcited interest.

Suddenly, however, something met her sight which riveted her attention; she grasped the paper more firmly, she sat upright instead of leaning back ; she pushed her hair away from her face as though it oppressed her, and then read the passage which had caught her notice once again more carefully. This was what it contained,—

" A shocking murder is reported as having taken place in the north of Ireland, hitherto comparatively free from the charge of agrarian outrage. The victim is a Mr. Brady, a gentleman of some property, and connected by marriage with several families of ancient lineage and high standing. The unfortunate gentleman was discovered about a mile from his own house quite dead, though still warm. A dispute about some land is supposed to have urged on his murderer. A man named Scott has been taken into custody; a stick with which the fatal blow was dealt, and known to have belonged to Scott, having been found near the spot. The unfortunate gentleman had not yet reached the prime of life. He leaves a widow and several children to deplore his untimely fate."

There are truths so terrible that the mind at first absolutely refuses to accept them, and like one in a dream with a stunned surprise, Grace Moffat read and re-read the paragraph, unable to realize its meaning.

Then suddenly the full horror of its statement broke upon her. It had come, then, this trouble, the prevision of which she now understood she had felt that morning when she and Mr. Hanlon walked over to the Castle Farm. It had come at a moment when she was least prepared for it, when her thoughts were far distant from Ireland ; when, much as she loved her own country, she was becoming reconciled to the ways and manners of another country ; when she was learning to like English people, and beginning, as the young always can do, to find an interest in the hopes, fears, and projects of those with whom she was thrown.

How the next half-hour was passed Grace never precisely knew. The servants, glad in that orderly household of an excitement of any kind, prepared and retailed many versions of how Marrables—Mrs. Hartley's highly respectable butler, who had a presence like a bishop and a face solemn and important as that of a parish clerk—hearing the bell ring violently hurried to the morning-room, where he found Miss Moffat standing in the middle of the apartment looking like death itself; how surprised out of his dignified deportment for once, he said before he was spoken to,—

" Gracious ! Miss, what has happened, and what is the matter ? "

To which she replied,—" Get me something;

I have had a great shock." He fetched her
wine and the housemaid water, and the lady's
maid smelling-salts and eau-de-cologne and a
fan ; whilst the butler suggested the propriety
of sending at once for a doctor.

"No," said Miss Moffat authoritatively, " I
shall be better soon ;" and she sat down and
leaned back and shut her eyes, the trio re-
garding her with interest, not unmixed with
awe the while.

Then almost directly she opened her eyes,
and looking at them one after the other, remarked,—

"It is not true, is it ? "

" No, Miss," answered Marrables promptly ;
his acquaintance with illness was slight, but
he had always heard sick people ought to be
humoured.

"Ah ! I forgot," said Miss Moffat wearily.
" Pour me out some wine and water, Marrables,
I will take it now ; and Taylor," turning to
Mrs. Hartley's maid, "I wish you would pack
up some dresses and linen for me ; I must go
to Ireland to-night."

"Yes, Miss."

"And directly Mrs. Hartley returns let me know."

"Mrs. Hartley is here now," exclaimed Marrables, and went out to meet his mistress, followed reluctantly by his fellow-servants.

Into the room came Mrs. Hartley dressed in all her bravery, with a face expressive of the utmost anxiety.

"What is all this, Grace, that Marrables has been frightening me with? Why, child, what has happened? You look as if you had seen a ghost."

For answer, Grace picked up the 'Times' and handed it to her friend, pointing out the paragraph she wished her to read. Marrables saw her do it, and it was not long before he had read the passage also.

"What are you thinking of doing?" asked Mrs. Hartley, drawing her out into the open air, and holding a parasol over her.

"I shall go to Ireland to-night," Grace answered.

"For what purpose?"

" Chiefly to be with Nettie, partly to see if anything can be done for Amos."

" You think he is guilty."

" I do not see that there can be any doubt of that. He must have been mad; but I suppose whether mad or not he will have to suffer for it all the same."

Mrs. Hartley paused. She took in the position at once ; she knew Grace's temperament, and she felt certain she would never rest content to remain inactive at such a juncture.

" Money can do a great deal," she remarked at last, " and influence more ; and in any case I know it will be a comfort hereafter for you to think both were brought to bear on this case. Yes, my love, I will not say a word to dissuade you from your intention ; I would offer to go with you myself if I thought I could be of any real assistance. Marrables shall accompany you as far as Dublin—there Mr. Nicholson can see to you. And, Grace, do not fret about the matter more than you can possibly avoid. A loophole may be found for Scott to creep through, and as for Nettie, I fancy she will be far happier as a widow than ever she was as a wife."

"Oh! do not say that," Grace entreated. "It was almost the first idea which occurred to me, and I hated myself for it."

"Well, we will not say anything about it then," agreed Mrs. Hartley, "although if he has left her comfortably off—" but here Miss Moffat stopped her ears and refused to listen. She was recovering from the first effect of the blow, but she could not bear to hear the tragedy discussed in this matter-of-fact, cool, business-like style.

Young people are occasionally somewhat unreasonable. It jarred against Grace's sensibilities to hear some two hours later the dinner-bell ring just as though Mr. Brady were not lying at Maryville stiff and cold, and Amos Scott not in Kilcurragh Gaol charged with his murder. Perhaps Mrs. Hartley guessed something of this, for she said,—

"Now, Grace, unless you eat I shall not allow you to go. Fasting may be all very well in its way, and I dare say it is, but it is not well when a young lady has a long journey before her, and the prospect of a considerable amount of work to follow."

Hearing which remark Mr. Marrables, who waited upon the ladies with his accustomed dignity, took especial care to fortify his system with a thorough good meal, and to provide against any casualties in the way of starvation by packing up a goodly supply of edibles, and laying the cellar likewise under contribution to a moderate though judicious extent.

After all, if the English are unimpulsive, they are useful; if they are undemonstrative, they are not heartless. Grace was forced to admit both these facts when she discovered everything she could possibly require packed up without a question being asked on the subject; when she found her travelling-dress laid out for her to don before dinner that she might not be obliged to hurry from table; when she saw the carriage brought round to a second, and beheld Marrables, after he had shut her and Mrs.

Hartley within, mount on the box beside the coachman with no more fuss than if he were merely going to attend his mistress to the station; when she heard Mrs. Hartley, who, as a rule, did not like shortening her meals, remark,—

"Now, my dear, I think it is time we were putting on our bonnets," and go off to prepare for a twelve miles' drive as if it were in the ordinary course of things for an elderly lady to consider her own ease so little.

These things all impressed Grace sensibly, as did one other little trifle. At the last moment it was discovered that by some oversight Miss Moffat's warm shawl had been left behind.

"Fetch my cloak out of the brougham," said Mrs. Hartley immediately, and, spite of her guest's remonstrances, she insisted on Grace taking it with her.

"Such magnificence!" exclaimed Miss Moffat, looking at the fur lining and the satin outside.

"Nonsense; it is old and worn, and shabby, but it will keep you warm. Good-bye now, my child—come back to me safe and sound —God bless you!" And the train was off.

CHAPTER IX.

GRACE VISITS MARYVILLE.

With much the same feeling as a Gipsy, who has been compelled to live for a time amongst the house-dwellers, returns to the camp on the common, to the savoury supper furnished gratuitously from his nearest neighbour's farmyard, to the bed on the green-sward, with heaven for a canopy and ferns for his pillow, so Grace, after a not disagreeable or uninstructive sojourn in the foreign land of England, beheld once more the fair shores and heard the familiar accents of her own country.

Home, after all, is home be it ever so homely ; and the tones and the voices familiar to childhood sound sweet after absence, let those tones and voices lack refinement though they may.

Grace had outgrown her prejudice against the English as affected. She had learned that their accent was as genuine and natural as the rougher tongue of her native land; but still just as a Londoner, coming south from the Land o' Cakes, thanks God when he reaches Carlisle to hear again something approaching a civilized language, so her heart warmed at sound of the familiar intonation. She was home again; she was amongst her own country people; she was no longer lost in the great country of England; she was a person of importance once more; she had ceased to be a princess in disguise,—back in the old familiar places, she was Miss Moffat of Bayview again.

From the moment she set foot in Dublin, she recognized that fact; and once for all I may as well state, it was pleasant to her. She had been but one of many in England; she was a person of importance in Ireland. She had

learned much near the head-quarters of civili-
sation, but she had not learned to be indifferent to the prestige given by wealth and
rank and being well known by repute even
beyond her county.

These weaknesses, which add so much to
happiness, but which usually develope themselves later in life, were with Grace an integral part of her nature. She was of the
soil; she was Irish and she loved everything
Irish. There might be things in the country
she could wish improved, but still the place
was home to her. And Grace's heart swelled
and her eyes filled with tears as she heard the
brogue floating around her, and those per-
suasive tones which in Dublin always seem
addressed only to one person, and that the
listener, fell upon her ear.

Dirty, picturesque, polite, plausible, un-
successful, they were her countrymen and
countrywomen; and for a moment, Grace, in
the excitement of her return, forgot the errand
which had brought her back, and said to
Mr. Nicholson in an access of enthusiasm,—

" How delightful all this is after England ! "

" It is very kind of you to say so, Miss Moffat," he replied. " For my part, I think London is the only place worth living in on earth."

" Oh ! fie," exclaimed Grace, " and you an Irishman ! "

" It is precisely because I am an Irishman that I say so," was the reply. " I have met with many English people who believe they should like always to reside in Dublin."

" I never have," and Grace sighed when she thought of Mrs. Hartley's openly expressed opinions.

Ere long, however, her enthusiasm toned down. She had not reached Mr. Nicholson's house before her thoughts were busy with the matter which had brought her to Ireland. Across the breakfast-table she talked to her companion about Amos Scott, and how it would fare with him.

" I fear badly," said that gentleman, who had heard all about the farmer during the time he spent at Bayview, and read the reports that followed after the murder, in the papers. "Everything seems against him. His animus was no secret, and his stick was found beside the dead man."

"Poor Amos," ejaculated Grace. "His wrongs have driven him mad."

"Neither wrongs nor madness will reconcile a north of Ireland jury to knocking a man over in the dark," said Mr. Nicholson sententiously. "His chance might have been better in the south or west."

"What do you think they will do to him?" asked Miss Moffat anxiously.

Mr. Nicholson paused for a moment, then he said,—

"I am afraid it will go against him, and if it does, unless he have powerful friends—"

"Oh!" she cried, "there is not one in all that part of the country but would speak for him. Every one knows how sorely he has been tried. Every one's sympathy must be with him—"

"Surely, Miss Moffat, your sympathies are not with him?" interposed Mr. Nicholson gravely. "Let Mr. Brady be what he might, his right to the land was undoubted. A man is not to be murdered because he asks for his own."

Having made which remark much in the interest of the servant, who, as is usual in Ireland, had both ears laid back to listen to the conversation of his betters, the lawyer relapsed into silence, leaving Grace to cogitate at her leisure over the plain truth contained in his sentence.

Her sympathies were with Amos Scott, but her common sense told her a man ought to be able to insist on having his own without paying for his temerity by his life.

Once again she was at sea, as every person is sooner or later who embarks on the study of Irish difficulties. "There was something rotten in the state of Denmark" she had long known. Dimly she was beginning to comprehend part of the rottenness lay in public feeling, popular prejudice, in that crass ignorance born of Romish supremacy, and nursed by self-asserting Dissent, till it might have puzzled a wiser than Solomon to say whether Catholic or Protestant were the most intractable—whether the senseless obedience of the south to its priests were worse than the bigoted intolerance of the north to every created being which differed in opinion from itself.

Every great virtue throws a shadow—the loftier the virtue the longer the shadow. Grace understood, who better?—the virtues of her hardworking, uncomplaining, patient, stubborn northern compatriots; but the dark shadows she had seen likewise; she was beginning to understand that the natives of no land are perfect, that God has conferred no more special patent of immunity from the taint of original sin on the poor than on the rich.

Though an enthusiastic, Grace was a thoughtful woman—a conjunction in one so quietly brought up, not merely possible, but probable, and the problem of humanity, which sooner or later troubles every one brought into contact with it, began to perplex her the first hour she again set foot in Ireland.

The same trouble which beset her is vexing

English philanthropists at the present day.
Even in happy England there is a cancer; who
shall adventure to cut it out? there is a worm at
the root; who shall dare turn up the ground,
and show where it is? There are doctors who
would palliate—there are men who would de-
stroy the upper branches—who would prune
and cut and lop and top the trees; but there
are none, unless, indeed, it may be a few brave
souls, who have wisdom enough and courage
sufficient to turn round and tell the lower
classes,—" The disease is in yourselves. We
cannot cure it unless you will consent to help
yourselves. You may lop and top for ever—
you may cut down an ancient aristocracy, and
try to dignify a mushroom nobility of your
own creation, but your labour will be for
nought, and your trouble loss utterly without
gain, for wherever the evil may have begun
it is with you it now lies. The rank and file
of the social army are utterly demoralised.
Each man wants to command. No man is
willing to obey. The spirit of discontent is
abroad. Work has become distasteful; in that

state of life in which God has placed him no human being seems satisfied to stay."

In one respect the fault of the Irish has always been that of resting satisfied too easily, and this idea was an integral part of Grace's faith. At the same time she, being at once clear-sighted and critical, could not avoid seeing her country people were satisfied easily, or indeed at all, only when the satisfaction was given in the way that pleased them ; that is to say, a dinner of fish, under certain conditions, was not objectionable, but a dinner, even off a stalled ox, unless it happened to be served exactly as they thought well, or in the place they saw fit to eat it, would not have met with their approval.

Had she not herself offered to Amos Scott the choice of farms as fertile, homesteads as substantial as that he could hope to hold no longer ; and had he not refused her kindness almost with scorn. He said he would have the familiar acres or none. He would have the home rendered dear by the mere passage of time, by the events which had taken place within its walls, or else a dry ditch and the stars of heaven shining down on him and his.   He would law and law and law until his last shilling was gone, in feeing men who could never put his wrong right on this earth ; he would fight every inch of the ground only to be beaten at last ; he said all this—what had come of it ?

That he was lying in gaol, waiting his trial for murder ; that, likely as not, he would walk out some morning on the scaffold—his grey hair floating in the wind—to end years of suffering, to expiate years of folly with his life.

Her sympathies were with him.   How would it fare with the wrong-doers, if no one had compassion for those who err ?   If she could help him, if she could save him, she would. To Mrs. Hartley she had said, and said as she believed truly, she must return to Ireland chiefly for Nettie's sake.   Now she was in Ireland, Grace could not conceal from herself the fact that she had come home as much in the interests of the accused as in those of Mr. Brady's widow.

" Poor Amos," she thought, " the gentry will be all against him.   They will forget what he suffered. They will remember only his sin."

Notwithstanding Mrs. Nicholson's entreaties, Grace made no longer stay in Dublin than it was possible to avoid. She longed to be in the north. It seemed to her she was needed there, and Mr. Nicholson, having been so fortunate as to find an acquaintance who was proceeding as far as Kilcurragh, put the heiress in his charge, and, it may as well be confessed with some misgivings as to how Grace would comport herself in so critical a position, saw her off.

"If you want my help," he said, and he felt quite certain she would, "I will come at an hour's notice."

Very gratefully she gave him her hand, and thanked him with one of her rare and wonderful smiles.

"A woman, if she had been portionless, to have driven a man to distraction," considered Mr. Nicholson, and he was right. An heiress is never so truly a woman as other women. Gold clothes her as with a garment, and it is a somewhat stiff robe in which to take her walks abroad.

Decidedly Grace would have been a more charming, even though a much less useful woman, had her face alone been her fortune.

As matters stood, however, she made friends so successfully with the elderly gentleman who was her travelling companion, that by the time they arrived at their journey's end, he was sufficiently interested in Amos Scott to assist her in finding his solicitor, who chanced to be a gentleman famous for making the best of bad cases—for getting off notorious vagabonds, for taking advantage of legal quibbles, and saving men's money and lives by the splitting of a legal straw.

"We are all friends here, I suppose," he said looking doubtfully at Grace's companion, whilst he stripped the feathers off a pen. "I may speak confidentially?"

"Most decidedly," Grace answered.

"I can do nothing for him," he remarked. "He will not trust me."

"How do you mean?" she asked.

"He says he is innocent. What can any human being do in the face of such an assertion?"

For a minute or two Grace sat silent. The idea was as new to her as obnoxious to Scott's lawyer. Hitherto it had never occurred to her that he would deny his guilt; but now— something—not born of reason or conviction, but a subtle instinct, prompted her to answer,

"If Amos Scott says he is innocent, you may believe him. I have known him since I was a child. At such a juncture he would not tell a lie."

The lawyer smiled.

"Believe me, Miss Moffat," he said, "the prospect of a halter has a wonderfully deterrent influence on the candour of most people."

"Perhaps," she replied; "but he would tell me the truth."

"Will you see him?" asked the other eagerly.

"Yes, certainly."

"And report the result of your interview to me?" he continued.

Only for an instant she hesitated, then she replied,—

"Word for word as far as I can recollect; what he says you shall hear."

"Then I may save him," he continued.

"If money—" began Grace, but he stopped her.

"I am not indifferent to money," was the reply, "but I never work for it alone. A thousand pounds paid down could never quicken my intellect as much as a perfect knowledge of a case. With Scott I am utterly at sea. He will not confide in me, and I do not know what to do for him. And the Assizes are close at hand, that is the worst of it."

"I shall see you again before the week is out," said Grace. "Meantime—" and she laid some notes on the table, which the lawyer folded up and handed to her once again.

"Money could do no more than I have tried to accomplish," he remarked. "When it is all over pay me if you will."

"Upon the whole, Miss Moffat," criticized

her travelling companion, "it seems to me the rogues have the best of it in this life. No honest man could find a lawyer like that," which is no doubt true. Perhaps it is part of the Eternal Justice to leave one world in which the rogues and the thieves and the plausible soft-spoken vagabonds have the best of it.

Spite of all the clergy tell us I am afraid, notwithstanding the hard lines many ragamuffins meet with, the paradise of sinners is earth.

Straight from Kilcurragh to Maryville drove Grace. Her travelling companion saw her and her slender luggage safely bestowed on the outside car, by which vehicle she elected to travel, and then made his farewell.

"Good-bye, Miss Moffat," he said; "I shall watch the progress of the case with interest and anxiety."

"He will tell the truth to me," she answered. And strong in this faith, she started on the long drive which lay before her.

Anxious to avoid Kingslough, and for a short time, at least, all contact with its inhabitants, she told the man to take a road lying a little inland which would, she knew, bring her out near the gates of Maryville.

It was a lovely evening, the sea lay like a mirror under the clear blue sky, the woods in the distance stood dark and green, mellowed by flushes of sunlight, that stole over them warm and bright; up and down the hillsides crept waving shadows and patches of golden light; the white cabins, nestling among fields where the wheat was already in the ear, looked as if they had every one been freshly whitewashed. Over the calm home landscape Grace gazed, tears dropping down in her heart the while; whilst her eyes gathered the peace and the loveliness of the familiar scene, her thoughts were concentrated on a grave in Kingslough churchyard. Life seemed to have begun for her in earnest at her father's death. Strangers dwelt under the remembered rooftree. To no hearth could she now creep close feeling it all her own. For others welcomes might sound, for others smiles might be wreathed, eyes brighten, tones grow softer, but for her with neither kith nor kin who cared that she was returning a lonely woman to comfort one almost as desolate as herself?

By the time she reached Maryville the sun had set, and the gloom of the dark avenue seemed to fall heavily upon her as they drove over the soft gravel, still wet from heavy rain which had fallen in the morning.

There was not a soul stirring about the place. At the lodge no one appeared, and the driver had to open the gates for himself. As they neared the house, it seemed like a building deserted.

Not a dog's bark broke the stillness, not a sound came through the evening air to prove that life was near at hand.

The man laid that day in his grave was no quieter than the place of which he had so lately been master. Through the hall the noise of Grace's knock echoed drearily. No city of the dead was ever more silent than Maryville on the first occasion that Miss Moffat set foot within its precincts.

Standing looking over the deserted lawn, Grace after a few moments heard the sound of footsteps coming apparently from some remote distance in the house. Across a stone passage, then along a wide corridor, then over the hall paved with black and white marble came that steady heavy tread. Next instant the door was opened sufficiently to admit of a head being thrust out to see who the intruder might be; a head, covered with luxuriant black hair, belonging to a woman from whose appearance Grace instinctively recoiled.

At sight of the visitor this woman opened the door a little wider, affording Miss Moffat a full view of a female of about seven or eight and twenty, tall, erect, bold.

Evidently she had been crying, but the traces of tears failed to soften the hard defiance of her dark eyes, or the tone in which she asked Grace what she was " pleased to want ? "

" Is Mrs. Brady within ? " inquired the visitor.

" She is," was the reply, uttered in an accent and with a manner as uncompromising as a north wind.

" Can I see her ? "

" It is not likely you can. Maybe you are a stranger, and have not heard what has happened."

" It is because I have heard," Grace answered, " that I am here. Be so good as to tell Mrs. Brady—"

" Who is it, Susan ? " called out a weak, querulous voice at this juncture. " No matter who it is, tell them I am in trouble and can see no one—remember that—no one ! "

" Not even Grace," answered her old friend. " Oh, Nettie ! I have travelled all the way from England to be with you. Let me come in and speak to you : let me stay—"

Before she had finished her sentence Mrs. Brady had crossed the hall and flung the door wide open.

" Grace ! Grace ! " she cried.

That was all. In a wordless agony she clung about the new-comer. She twined her arms around her, she laid her head on her shoulder, but she never cried nor sobbed. The years fraught with agony inconceivable, seemed to have taken the power of weeping from her.

"This is the first time she has come out of her room since—" began she of the black hair in explanation, but Mrs. Brady stopped her.

"Don't!" she said in that faint irritable voice, which spoke volumes to Grace of the sufferings she had endured. "I cannot bear to talk," she went on addressing her friend. "If you stay, if you really want to stay, you must never speak to me of it or him. Will you promise?"

"I never will unless you wish me to do so," Grace answered readily, scarcely realizing how difficult she might find it to keep her word.

"Where will I put the portmantle?" inquired the car-driver, breaking across the conversation with an abruptness which one at least of the trio felt to be a relief.

It was almost dark inside the house—so dark that Grace, unable to see the contents of her purse, stepped out into the twilight to pay the man.

"Can I get a drop of water for my horse, Miss?" he asked as she counted the money into his hands, and turning she repeated the

question to the servant who stood in the doorway.

"Not here," answered the woman. "The
men are gone, and the dogs are loose. There
is a stream crosses the road less than a mile
up it; the beast can drink his fill there."

Never before—never in the whole of her
life had Grace heard so inhospitable a sentence
uttered. Involuntarily it caused her to double
the amount of the man's own gratuity, and to
say to him in a low voice,—

"They are in great distress of mind here;
perhaps you know."

"Yes, Miss, I know," was the reply; but
Grace felt there was no sympathy in his tone,
and she turned to re-enter the house with a
conviction that even the circumstances of Mr.
Brady's death had failed to awaken popular
sympathy in his behalf.

"Where is Mrs. Brady?" she asked, peer-
ing through the twilight in search of Nettie,
who was, however, nowhere visible.

"She's gone back to her room; if you want
her, you'll have to go there after her. She

has never come down till to-night. She has not been to say quite right in her head ever since."

" Perhaps she would rather be alone ? "

"I don't think it will make any differ one way or the other," was the somewhat contemptuous answer which decided Grace on at once making her way to Nettie.

"Which is her room ? " she inquired.

"Right opposite you when you get to the head of the stairs ; " and thus directed, Grace without ceremony crossed the hall, ascended the staircase, and joined her friend.

She found Nettie pacing the apartment with slow, measured steps. Up and down, down and up, she marched like some animal on a chain, hopelessly, helplessly, wearily. Suddenly she stopped in this exercise.

" You ought not to stay here, Grace. I am no company for anybody now."

"If I had wanted company I should have stayed where I was," Grace answered. " I came here to see if I could not be of use to you, and I shall remain till I am quite satisfied I cannot be of any ! "

" No one can help me," said Nettie deliberately. Then finding Grace kept silence, she went on hurriedly to ask,—

" What are you thinking of ? "

" I was thinking, dear—" the words came softly through the darkness—" that God in His own good time will help you."

" He cannot," was the reply, spoken sharply and quickly.

" We shall see," and Grace sat down by one of the windows, while Nettie resumed her purposeless walk, backwards and forwards, forwards and backwards enough to drive a bystander to madness.

After a time the door opened.

" I have made you some tea, mem. Will you come down or will I bring it up to you ? "

Nettie never answered. Neither by sign nor token did she give evidence of having heard a word.

" I will come down," said Grace after a moment's pause, sufficient to permit Mrs. Brady to reply if she would. " Should you not like a light, Nettie ? " she asked with a

natural hesitation about making such a suggestion in another person's house.

"I hate light," was the answer.

"How long has she been like that?"
whispered Miss Moffat as the door closed
between her and the blue-eyed, golden-haired
Nettie of the long-ago past."

"Ever since that night; except cold water,
she has not had bite or sup in her lips for the
last five days."

"Where are the children?"

"I asked some of the neighbours to take
them till—till—it was all over."

There was an instant's break in her voice.
Next minute it was cold and hard and ringing
as ever.

In the small ante-room where Mr. Brady
had received the Rileys, Grace found tea prepared, and she sat down to it with what
appetite she might.

She had been delicately nurtured, and the
cup of coarse blue delft, the dark brown sugar,
the battered tray, the black-handled knife, the
smoked teapot, repelled her the moment she
set eyes on the repast.

But she forced herself to eat. She had come to be useful, and she was determined to let no fastidious niceties cumber her at first starting. Her greatest trial was the woman, who after a grudging fashion strove to make her welcome. Grace's experience had never previously brought her even mentally in contact with a person of the kind, but her instinct told her there was something wrong about dark eyes and darker hair; that if everything were right she and Nettie ought not to be under the same roof, with a person against whom every nerve seemed to be at war, whose very presence was a trial, whose interest in the late master of Maryville had evidently been very close and very great. By the light of the solitary candle with which her banquet-table was illumined, Grace, quick as is the nature of her sex, took in the personal appearance and attire of the solitary domestic Maryville seemed to boast.

Not an ill-looking woman; but hard, bold, bad—bad decidedly—one with whom wickedness had not prospered. Grace looked at her poor brown-stuff gown, scanty and ill-fitting, but covering a magnificent figure; at the poor attempt at mourning made in a little black neckerchief drawn round her throat and pinned in front of the half-high dress; at her hands red and hard with work, to grasp, dimly it might be but sufficiently, the fact sin had not paid this creature high wages for the loss of all women hold dear.

The man was dead. She had wanted to ask many questions, but with this idea before her and others looming behind, Grace could ask no question of her companion, who, comprehending that without a word of explanation the other knew her position, hardened herself and decided she would make this stranger's stay unpleasant if she could.

Understanding this in a vague uncertain fashion, Grace said,—

"I suppose you do not know who I am. Mrs. Brady and I are old friends, and I have come from England to be with her in this affliction. I used to live near Kingslough; my father was Mr. Moffat of Bayview."

"I have heard tell of you both," was the

reply sullenly spoken. "You'll have come over to help Amos Scott as well as to see Mrs. Brady, I'm thinking."

To which speech Miss Moffat deemed it prudent to make no reply.

CHAPTER X.

A RAY OF LIGHT.

NOT all Grace's persuasions could induce Mrs. Brady on the following morning to touch any breakfast. By special request Miss Moffat had been permitted to pass the night in a dressing-room opening into Nettie's apartment, and until overpowered by weariness she fell into a broken sleep, she heard the widow tossing from side to side, moaning now and then, at intervals breathing many sighs, but weeping never.

With her own hands Miss Moffat made her a tiny morsel of toast, and took that and a cup of tea to her bedside; but Nettie refused to eat, not querulously or with any effusion of

manner, but with a settled determination difficult to hope to sway.

Nevertheless, her friend thought she would
try. "Dear Nettie," she said, "you ought to
eat."

"I cannot; it would choke me," was the
reply.

"I am afraid you will bring on an illness."

"Oh! if I could only die," and she buried
her face in the pillow.

Grace went downstairs again.

As has been already stated her knowledge of
mortal, physical, or deep mental sickness was
not large; and if her knowledge of the latter
had been, she might well have felt puzzled
how to deal with Nettie.

After her breakfast she sat down for a few
minutes to think, and whilst she was deep in
meditation Susan entered.

"The mistress would take nothing, then,"
she remarked, looking at the tray Grace had
carried all unavailingly to Mrs. Brady.

"No."

"I thought you wouldn't get her to eat. I

have tried her hard enough, I can tell you. You don't seem to have been hungry yourself," she went on, glancing at the dish of bacon swimming in grease and the new-laid eggs that, poached in fat, floated in company with the unsavoury-looking slices.

"I was not," answered Miss Moffat.

"It is not a heartsome place to come to, you're thinking, likely," suggested the woman.

"I was thinking what I could do for Mrs. Brady," Grace replied. "She ought to have something. Is there any wine in the house?"

"There is whisky," was the answer.

Grace groaned mentally. "I wonder if she would take a little milk," she said audibly.

"You can try. Will I bring you some?"

There was a secret triumph in the tone, as though she suspected the attempt would prove futile. And she was right. Nettie would have nothing but water. Of that she drank incessantly.

"I am parched," she said in answer to Grace's remonstrances. "My lips are so dry they bleed;" and as she removed her handkerchief from them, Grace saw it was stained with crimson spots.

What would Grace not have given for Mrs. Hartley's counsel? Good women, and kind and true, lived at Kingslough, but somehow she felt at that juncture Mrs. Hartley's hard worldly sense would prove more useful than all the well-meant sympathy amiable but incompetent people could offer.

Besides, Nettie herself would have none of Kingslough, either in the way of pity or help.

All the morning Maryville was besieged with callers, notes, cards, and inquiries.

"They can come now," said Nettie bitterly, as she watched car and carriage and messenger depart unsatisfied. "They think I can go back and take the old up where I left off that morning. They do not know; how should they?"

Dinner-time arrived. With a bang, Susan set down on one side of the table at the other side of which Grace sat writing, a dish of potatoes piled high and another of herrings floating in a fresh sea of grease.

"Maybe it's not good enough for you," said the woman, with a sneer, "but it's all there is in the house."

"You mistake," said Grace; "it is quite good enough for me, but I do not think it is anything like good enough for Mrs. Brady." And she took her place at table whilst Susan flounced out of the room only to turn back and inquire whether she would " be plazed to drink water or milk."

Had she followed Mrs. Hartley's instructions Grace would have said water. As it was, the national partiality for milk common to the Irish ladies at that period, and which perhaps with the moist climate had share in their lovely complexions, extinguished all English lights, and so she chose the latter, thereby mollifying Susan, who thought " she might not be so stuck-up after all, maybe."

Of potatoes and milk Grace made her meal with relish, it must be confessed, and spite of her sorrow. The potatoes were capital, the milk rich. The herrings she could not fancy, the lake of slowly congealing fat in which they reposed effectually warned her from them. While she ate she thought, "Let Susan be what she would, or perhaps would not, she, Miss Moffat, could not put that wrong right if she kept her at arms' length for ever. On the whole, had she not better try to conciliate this woman, who, spite of her position, seemed friendly to Nettie? "Perhaps," thought Grace, "because she knows if this door closes behind her, none other would open to receive her."

There were not many women who dared even think of adopting a conciliatory policy under such circumstances; but in many ways Grace's position was exceptional.

After all, what is the good of virtue if it be not sufficiently certain of its own standing to walk just once and away on the same side of the road with vice, and refrain from drawing its skirts decorously around it?

Grace's virtue, at all events, was made of sufficiently strong stuff to risk all the results of such a companionship. She hated the sin she felt had been done, as probably those to

whom the nature of sin is almost a mystery
alone are able—with an abhorrence, a detestation, a contempt, a loathing, akin to the feelings with which a man who had bathed
from his earliest youth might look upon a
disease produced by filth, and the lack of all
ordinary physical cleanliness ; but—black tan-
gled hair, unkempt, unbraided, bold eyes, insolence, brazen defiance notwithstanding—she
was sorry for the sinner.

Where vice flaunts past dressed in the latest
fashion, driving a lovely pair of ponies, assum-
ing the most recent fashionable manner whether
that manner be modest or forward, we may
call it picturesque, and forget, if we choose,
the ghastly death's head lurking beneath the
rouge and paint and powder plastered on the
face of Sin's last successful child ; but when
we come to see some of Sin's despised daughters, some of those who have been cut off by
their unjust parent with less even than the
traditional shilling, I think the observer must
be less than man or woman—more fiend than
either can prove on occasion—who shall fail to

consider for what inconceivably small wages the devil gets immortal souls to work his ends.

If *his* employés would strike, what an involuntary lock-out from Hell here and Hell hereafter the world should witness!

" Susan," began Miss Moffat, as the handmaiden having piled plate and vegetable dish on the top of the herrings, was about to remove the dinner appointments on the extemporised tray,—"do not you think Mrs. Brady ought to see a doctor?"

" I think it's time she saw somebody," agreed Susan.

" Would not it be well to send one of the men with a note to Mr. Hanlon, asking him to call?"

" It's no use," answered Susan shaking her head. " Mr. Hanlon he came up the day of the inquest; he had to come, and after the crowner was gone he wanted to see mistress. In course, I asked him to step in here and told her, and you'd have thought she'd have taken my head off. I was glad enough to get out of the room.

I would not like to be the one who should tell her Mr. Hanlon was here again." .

"Why, I thought she always liked him," said Grace fairly puzzled.

"I can't say for that, it was hard to tell who Mrs. Brady liked or did not like—she is a mighty secret woman in her ways, but the master hated him and forbid him the house. Most like she minds all that."

"Poor Nettie, how fond she must have been of him after all!" murmured Grace, speaking her thoughts out loud.

"Fond of the master, is it you mean!" asked Susan. "Fond of him; that she wasn't, that she could not be, I'll take my Bible oath. Why, Miss—" and in her energy she banged the herrings and superstructure on the table again—"he treated her worse nor a slave. If it had not been for the children, she'd have gone over and over and over again. I have seen it in her face when she has been sitting beside the fire, thinking, thinking; or when maybe she has left the room after giving him one look. He's gone and there's no need for us to send the bad word after him; but no black negro ever had a worse time of it than the woman that's now a widow; and whatever she is fretting about—and if I was you Miss, I would not trouble my head concerning that matter—it is not her murdered husband."

"I am afraid you are not fond of Mrs Brady," suggested Grace. Perhaps the exact speech the unities might have suggested at such a crisis would not have been composed of the same or even similar words, but certainly an astute lawyer or a clever worldly woman would have put just the same question.

"An' saving your presence, Miss, who could be fond of her?" inquired Susan. "She's secret as the grave He might beat or starve or blackguard her as he liked, and she answered never a word. Never to one did she come for pity or help. I have heard them say Miss, old women, not like me, that over and over again they wanted to talk with her about her trouble, and she put them back. She was that proud Miss, flesh and blood could not thole her."

" Proud," Grace repeated, and she looked at the room, she glanced at the table.

"Ay, just proud," was the answer; "folks are often as proud of the things they want to have as of those they have got, and if they can't get all they want they turn sulky, just—just as she did," finished Susan, and without leaving Grace time for a reply, she took up the herring-dish and its belongings and disappeared.

When an hour afterwards she returned to claim the table-cloth, Miss Moffat had vanished.

Over the fields she was gone to visit Mrs. Scott. Now making her way across a meadow where, as is the Irish fashion, the hay had been gathered into about twenty small stacks, hay ropes binding the grass together; now treading lightly between potatoe rigs, now skirting a field of oats or barley, she came at length by a different route to any she had heretofore traversed to the homestead of the Castle Farm.

Straight into the kitchen Grace walked. Upstairs she heard the sound of movement and voices, and upstairs after knocking vainly on the dresser she proceeded.

A stifled shriek was the first sound which greeted her, the next was,—

"Miss Grace, go down again into the open air. And may God Himself preserve you from all evil. We have got the faver."

Sound of dread in Ireland! If there be a cowardly spot in the nature of Irish men and women even at the present day, it is their blind, unreasoning dread of infection.

Reared amongst those who held this horror, Grace at sound of Mrs. Scott's news involuntarily drew back. Next instant she stood by Reuben's bedside.

The lad was dying. Even her inexperience grasped that; and falling on her knees and burying her face in the coverlet, she wept tears she had been longing to shed ever since she entered Maryville.

"Miss Grace," it was the mother who spoke and touched her, "ye can't save him. Why should ye kill yourself?"

"And you?" asked Grace, looking at mother and friend.

"We are in the hands of God," was the reply.

"So am I," said Miss Moffat, and took the lad's white fingers in her own.

"Who is attending him," she asked.

"Mr. Hanlon—who but him? He had a right to do all he could for us; and I'll say that, in his benefit, he has done it.

"Why was it his right?" asked Grace, ignoring all the rest of the sentence save that which jarred on her ear.

"Because him, and men like him, made the good man what—what— There, God help us, Miss Grace! Go away or you'll be hearing me raving worse than my poor lad did when first he lay bad, and likely be taken yourself."

"I am not afraid," said Grace, but she moved towards the door as she spoke. "Mrs. Scott, I shall see Amos to-morrow I hope; what am I to tell him?"

"Tell him what you've seen, Miss Grace."

"And what else ?" asked her visitor.

"I don't just understand. Oh ! yes, I do. Downstairs if you please, Miss. I'll follow you."

In the sunlight Grace waited for her to come down, and involuntarily as she looked at the flood of golden light in which the landscape was steeped, she could not help thinking that as the rain falleth on the just and the unjust, so the sun shines on the happy and the miserable.

Whilst she was vainly trying to solve this great problem of nature's lack of sympathy, Mrs. Scott joined her, keeping at a respectful distance.

"I know what you mean, Miss Grace," began the woman, who had grown old suddenly ; " but, between you and me and him, it's no use talking of innocency if the other thing be guiltiness. He did it, and if I had been in his place, I'd ha' done it myself."

These people—neither the man nor the woman—nor men nor women like them, were likely to take refuge in falsehood, and conviction entered Grace's heart at that moment. If Amos had sinned, he would have told how it all came about ere now. Had his been the hands that struck his enemy down, he would have waited for no warrant but given himself up, and with obstinate honesty endured the consequences of his guilt.

Or it might be that in the natural terror induced by the accomplishment of such a deed, and the horror of the consequences certain to ensue, he would have fled. Either the sturdy endurance or the frantic fear would not have been out of keeping with the hard, stubborn, straightforward nature — but resolutely to maintain his innocence even to his own lawyer—to offer no explanation as to whether the blow was dealt in cold blood or after bitter altercation—Grace could not reconcile such a line of conduct with anything she could remember of Scott, and out of the fulness of her heart she spoke, "As certainly as you stand there I believe Amos never killed that man."

"Do you think you'll make a jury believe

that, Miss Grace?" asked Mrs. Scott, holding a blue-checked apron to her face, down which tears were coursing. Well, well—one trouble is almost driven out by another—when Reuben's gone, there'll be no one to think about but the master."

In this she chanced to be mistaken, however. When Reuben was gone, she herself lay fighting for dear life with the fever which had passed by her husband; leaving him, so most people said, for a worse fate than death by the visitation of God.

CHAPTER XI.

IN THE NIGHT-WATCHES.

BEFORE Miss Moffat had nearly reached Maryville, Susan met her.

"It went out of my head, Miss," she began, "to tell you they had the fever at the farm. You have been there most like."

"Yes; and seen the lad who appears to be dying."

"What will we do now," asked Susan in an access of despair, "the children have come home?"

"Well, what of that?"

"What of that!" repeated the woman, scornfully, "like as not you'll have brought the fever home in your clothes with you."

Grace stopped. It was a serious loss to her as a woman that she had never been with illness, and knew little or nothing about it, and now unwittingly she had run the risk of doing a very terrible wrong,—bringing infection into another person's house, amongst another person's children.

" Oh ! I am so sorry," she exclaimed, unheeding the contemptuous inflection of Susan's voice; "what can we do; what ought I to do ?"

"You had better take off your outside things, and give them to me to hang up in the air," was the reply uttered in a mollified tone. " I will bring down your wrapper; and then if you throw your other clothes into water, maybe no harm will come of it. But don't go talking to the mistress till you've changed."

" I will not," promised Miss Moffat, and she tried to keep her word, for when Mrs. Brady called to her querulously, Grace answered,—

"Wait for a few minutes, I will be with you directly."

"I want you now."

"I cannot come. I have been to the Castle Farm, and Reuben is ill with fever; and I must get rid of all possible chance of carrying infection before I see any one."

"I do not care about infection," answered Nettie.

"Well, if you do not I do," retorted Grace, and she essayed to bolt her door; but as is not uncommon, even now in Ireland, all means of secure fastening were either broken or inoperative. "Dear Nettie," she went on, "do not come near me; for the sake of the children, if not for your own, keep away."

But Mrs. Brady resolutely had her will.

"Who did you see at the Castle Farm?" she asked.

"Mrs. Scott and Reuben. Nettie do be persuaded, and go away. If you or any of the children caught this fever, I should never forgive myself."

"We will not catch fever any one of us,"

answered Mrs. Brady. "I want to hear about the Scotts. What does Mrs. Scott say? You know what I mean.

"About Amos?" Grace suggested; "what can she say. Do not let us talk of it, Nettie."

"I must talk of it. Are you not going to see him, Grace?"

"Yes; but I did not intend to tell you."

"Why not? I want you to go. I want to hear every word he speaks to you."

"Nettie, you are ill," said Miss Moffat, noticing the flush on her friend's thin cheeks, the brightness of her eyes, and the parched dryness of her lips; "is there nothing you could fancy, dear; nothing I could get that might tempt you to eat?"

Mrs. Brady shook her head; then said with a faint smile,—

"I will try to eat something if you promise to tell me word for word all Amos says to you."

"How can I do so, you being what you are?" Grace replied.

"I am the most miserable wretch on earth,"

Nettie exclaimed. "My heart is breaking, Grace, and you will not do the simplest thing to try and ease it."

"Nettie dear, how can you ask me?" pleaded Miss Moffat. "I do not love you less because I refuse to betray any confidence the unhappy man may put in me."

"Do you think I want him hung?" inquired Nettie. "Do you think I should not be glad to hear he had got off safe? I tell you, if laying down my own life could procure his acquittal, I would cheerfully do it."

"You certainly must be insane," said Grace, with the quiet force of conviction; "however, to humour you I promise this, that I will repeat as much as I can of our conversation, although I should have thought this the very last subject on which you would have wished to hear me speak."

"Should you?" exclaimed Nettie. "Well, that only shows how mistaken even clever people may be sometimes. Hush! Here comes that woman!" and Mrs. Brady slipped back into her own room, closing the door softly behind her.

Faithful to her promise Nettie did try to swallow something, but the attempt proved almost a total failure.

"It chokes me, dear," she said almost humbly to her friend. "I wish—I wish I could have something to quiet me a little. Don't you think," she added wistfully, "that old Dr. Girvan, who has seen so many people in trouble, might think of something that would do me good?"

"He shall try," answered Grace; and she sent a messenger for him.

When the old man arrived he shook his head, called Nettie 'poor girl'; felt her pulse, said the shock had been too much for her; advised that she should leave Maryville as soon as possible; expressed his intention of sending her a soothing mixture, and went away believing he understood Mrs. Brady's case.

"Ah!" said Nettie after he had gone, "if these doctors when they listen to our hearts' throbbing could only tell what is really passing in them, how we should dread their coming!"

"Dear, do try to keep yourself quiet," expostulated Grace, and Nettie obediently kept silence.

Another restless night, as Grace heard; so restless that Grace rose and taking the child Nettie had insisted on having to sleep with her away, put the little creature into her own bed, and kept watch by Mrs. Brady till the next morning.

"Grace," said the widow turning her face towards her friend, and stroking the hand that held hers so tenderly, "you are too good to me by far; but some day I do not think you will be sorry to remember all you have done for me."

"Darling, I am only too thankful to be able to do anything," was the reply, and Grace pillowed the once beautiful face upon her arm; and whilst Nettie slept fitfully, looked at the lines trouble had graven on the forehead she could remember, as if it were only a day previously, white and smooth and unmarked by even a trace of care.

Without much trouble Amos Scott's solicitor had been able to obtain permission for Miss Moffat to see her old friend. In Kilcurragh it was talked of as a nine days' wonder that a young lady of fortune and position should so far demean herself as to pay a visit to a common murderer; for according to general procedure the public had already tried and condemned the suspected man.

If people were not very much concerned about Mr. Brady's death, they were at least very greatly infuriated against Amos Scott.

"No man's life," they said, "would be safe if the farmer was allowed to get off,—if those who considered themselves injured were suffered to take the law into their own hands and revenge themselves as they pleased." With much more to the same effect, which Miss Moffat did not hear, and which would not have greatly affected her had she heard.

Never before had Grace felt so much shocked at the change a short time is capable of effecting as when she beheld Amos Scott.

He was worn almost to skin and bone; and there was a sad, weary, despairing look in his face that might well touch the heart of a woman who had known him in his prime of health and hope and prosperity.

There was a gentleness in his manner she had never perceived before. It seemed almost as though he had already passed through the gates of death and dropped the rude garments that concealed his finer and higher nature at the portals.

"Miss Grace; Miss Grace, why did you ever come to a place like this," were his first words. "If the master had been alive he would not have suffered it."

"Very probably not," she answered. "He would have come for me in that case; now I am alone, I have no one."

"Why did you demean yourself for the likes of me?" he asked.

"I am not demeaning myself," she replied, "and I came to see you because, guilty or innocent, I cannot forget the past."

"I am not guilty, Miss Grace."

"On your solemn word, Amos."

"If I was standing before my Maker, face to

face, as I believe I soon shall," he said rising, and lifting his hand reverently above his head, "I am not guilty in deed of the black villain's death. I do not go so far as to say," he went on, dropping his hand and resuming his seat, like one too weak to remain long standing, "I never wished him dead. I have often; and even now I can hardly feel sorry that he has been struck down. I have been a murderer in my heart, Miss Grace; I don't deny it. Many and many a night when I have been tramping home through the wet and the mud—empty of food and sick with sorrow,—I have thought if I could just hear he had taken the fever, or broken his neck, or been upset and drowned, I could have made myself content to leave the old place—and Ireland,—and go away to the country I said I never could thole to be banished to. But now," he added after an expressive pause, "I shall never have the chance; I shall never go anywhere but from here to the Court, and from the Court back here; and from here to—"

He covered his face.   A man may be brave enough, and yet weak as a child when he tries to speak of an ordeal such as this.

For a minute Grace did not speak; she could not for the tears she was trying to restrain.   Then she said, " Amos ! " and he lifted his head.

" Yes, Miss Grace."

" Before God you are innocent ? "

" I have said so once, Miss ; there is no need in my saying so twice ; for if you don't believe me at my first telling, you won't believe me at my second."

" I beg your pardon," she said gently, " I did believe you the first time.   I ought not to have tried to make assurance doubly sure.   More than that, before I ever came here I felt you were innocent, and if it is possible for me to save you, I will do it."

" Miss Grace," he answered, " you mean kindly, but you may be doing me a deadly hurt.   I have been facing certain death since I came here, and its bitterness is almost past.

If you drag me back, even for a bit, I must go through it all again."

It was a homely way of expressing the cruelty of raising false hopes; but Grace understood his meaning perfectly.

"I am rich," she faltered, feeling the error she had committed.

"Money won't do it," he answered.

"I have many friends possessed of influence."

"Influence can't save me. There is only one thing could help me, Miss Grace; and I need not trouble you with talking about that, because I know no more than the child still unborn who killed the man. I have sat here and gone over, and over, and over the story, and can make neither head nor tail of it. All I am sure of is, I had no act or part in the murder; and how my stick came to be where they say it was found is beyond me, for I lost it the night before; and I never was near the divisional road at all."

"What does Mr. D'Almarez say?" asked Miss Moffat."

" He says nothing, except 'tell me the truth,' as if a man in my strait would be likely to tell his attorney a lie."

" And what does he think about your having lost your stick ?"

" He just thinks I never lost it, because when he asked me about the places I had been the day before, I couldn't mind. I have been that perplexed, Miss, since Lady Jane died, my memory won't serve me as it used."

" But surely, Amos, with trying, you might recollect."

" I have minded a good many. I was at Rosemont to try to get speech of Mr. Robert; and at the office; and at the Glendare Arms, where a stranger man, seeing I was in trouble, treated me to a glass, bad luck to it ! for I had not broken my fast, and the liquor got into my head; and I said things about Brady they're going to bring up again me at the trial; and then I stopped at a heap of places besides, but I can't mind just where, except that at the last I called at Hanlon's surgery for some stuff for the lad. I didn't forget that, because he went on at me for having had too much, and made me mad because he wouldn't believe me I had only had one glass to overcome me—me—who could once have taken off half-a-dozen without winking.

"And on the day of the ——, on the day when Mr. Brady was killed?" Grace persisted.

"Well, Miss, I was that beat from the day before, I did not stir out till evening; and I would not have gone then, but the wife she would have me go to Kingslough and tell the doctor the boy was worse. So I went there and he was out, and I left my message; and in the ordinary way I should have come straight home, but I thought I would go round by Mark Lennon's, and tell his daughter we had a letter from him she's promised to; but before I got there I turned that bad and weak, I thought to make my home as fast as I could, and so came across the fields and the Red Stream; and they make that a charge against me too, Miss Grace, because, as you know, the colour of the clay there is the same as the colour of the clay in the water alongside the divisional where Brady was found."

In spirit, Grace groaned. She believed the man was speaking truly, but what jury on earth would believe it also ! There was not a point in his favour. Every statement he made told against him. He could not say where he lost his stick. He could not say where he had been to lose it. He could not account for his time after he left Kingslough on the night of the murder. As to the place where he got the mud found on his clothes, there was only his own word, and of what value is the word of an accused man. Even his own wife imagined him guilty. No one in the world, save Grace Moffat, imagined it within the bounds of possibility that, though circumstantial and internal evidence were all against him, he might yet be innocent; and it was just on the board that had she lived in Ireland for the previous twelve months, and seen his animus to Mr. Brady growing day by day, she might have believed him guilty too.

" All I can say," she remarked, as she rose

to leave, "is this; you shall have the best counsel money can procure."

"Thank you kindly, Miss," he answered, "but, as I said before, money can't do it, and man can't do it, let him be the best ever stepped in shoe leather; and if God does not do it, and in these later days, as our minister used to say, he has not seen fit to work visible miracles, I must suffer, Miss Grace; that is all. I have made my mind up to that now *he* is dead, as I never could to giving up the farm while he was living."

"Amos," said Miss Moffat, "do not let what your minister said impress you too much. God does still work miracles, or what seem miracles to us; and if he sees fit he will clear you from this."

"And if He does not see fit, Miss Grace, I must just thole what He sends; that is all. You can say that to the wife if you have a chance. Do you happen to know, Miss, how it is with Reuben?"

For a moment Grace faltered; then she said,—

"Whatever else you are spared to see in this world I am afraid—" she paused, and he calmly finished the sentence.

"I won't see him. Well then, Miss, it may be we shall meet all the sooner, Reuben and me, when he will know that wrongfully blood-guiltiness was laid to my charge."

Mr. D'Almarez made no secret of his chagrin at the result of this interview, and it taxed his politeness sorely to listen to Miss Moffat's account of it with even ordinary patience.

He had hoped that to her Scott would speak openly. He had expected to obtain some information which might bring the crime under the head of accident rather than design, and enable him to fight for a verdict of man-slaughter instead of murder. It was known to every one in the county that Mr. Brady had not treated the man well; and if Scott could only be got to state what actually passed on the last occasion he and his enemy ever met, the lawyer felt something might be done, supposing the blow had been struck without premeditation, and that high and passionate words had preceded it.

If a jury could be argued or coaxed into believing Scott did not leave his home with the deliberate intention of murdering Mr. Brady, the man's chance was by no means hopeless; and there was this in his favour, that the owner of Maryville had actually on the day of the murder started to go to Dublin, although for some unexplained reason he failed to continue his journey, so that it was unlikely Scott could have expected to meet him near the Castle Farm.

On the other hand, it was against the accused that he knew Mr. Brady intended to eject him from the house—that he had publicly stated, " Brady should never come into it alive," and that he expressed his intention of sticking to the old place even if it was pulled down about his ears.

Still, considering what Mr. Brady had been, and the amount of fancied or real injury he inflicted on Amos, considering that the one man had always been a dishonest reprobate,

and the other a hard-working decent, well-
conducted fellow, who never cheated a neighbour of a halfpenny; that he had a son down
in fever, and children clamouring for bread;
that he might well be nearly distraught
with want of food, and mental anguish; considering what a picture a clever barrister
might fill in from these outlines, Mr. D'Almarez did not despair of doing something for
Scott, if only he could be induced to confess.
And now it seemed he did not intend to confess; and the lawyer, chafing with irritation,
had to sit and listen to a woman's maunderings
about innocence and Scott's religious utterances and other matters of the same kind, all
of which Mr. D'Almarez mentally summed up
in one word, "Rubbish!"

"It is all very well, Miss Moffat" he said,
when she finished, "for Scott to talk goody
twaddle—excuse the expression—to a lady or
a parson; but that sort of thing will not go
down with a judge or a jury. He mistakes
his position; the period has not yet arrived for
that kind of conversation. Time enough for

religious exercises when he has done with lawyers and been turned over to the chaplain. You must pardon my plain speaking. The only hope there is of saving Scott lies with himself, and if he will persist in trying to hoodwink me and playing at this foolish game of hide-and-seek with his own attorney, I am afraid there is not a chance of saving him."

"But, Mr. D'Almarez," pleaded Grace, "suppose the man has nothing to tell, suppose he is not guilty, suppose he has really tried to make his peace with God, expecting nothing from man, and that every word he said to me to-day were true, the natural expression of a broken and a contrite heart, in which not a hope, so far as this world is concerned, still lingers?"

The lawyer smiled. It was very right and proper, of course, for a lady to talk in this strain, but it was a style of conversation for which he himself did not much care, and very possibly had Miss Moffat been older and uglier and poorer, he might not have listened to it even with the amount of politeness he evinced.

"I cannot suppose an impossibility," he answered. "Your own kindness of disposition and Scott's solemn assertions have, you must allow me to say, blinded your judgment. If you exercise it you will understand that it is a simple impossibility for Scott to be innocent. He may be innocent of intentional murder, and that is the only point we can try to make in his favour, but his hands are not clean in the matter as he tries to make us believe.

"Remember the hatred he entertained for Mr. Brady, recollect all he had suffered through him, recall the expressions he was habitually in the practice of using concerning him, the threats he uttered not farther back than the day before the murder, and then pass on to the murder itself. Mr. Brady is found dead in a lonely road leading straight to the Castle Farm. He has been killed by a blow, and that blow it is not disputed must have been dealt by a stick, and that stick one belonging to Scott, which is found at a little distance as if flung away in a panic. According to Scott's own account he was

not in the divisional road at all that night, and
yet it was the most direct route back from Mr.
Hanlon's, where he admits he called. He says
he started to go round by Lennon's, but he
never went there. He says he lost his stick
on the previous day, but he does not know
where or how, and he cannot even remember
the places at which he stopped, or whether he
missed his stick before his return home, or
whether he ever missed it till it was found
after the murder.

"Further, admitting he did lose it, there is
no particular reason why he should not have
found it again. Nor does the evidence against
him stop even at this point. It is certain his
clothes were wet, and stained with clay of a
reddish colour. The banks and bed of the
stream running beside the divisional road
are, as you know, of that description. Depend
upon it, Miss Moffat, Scott is throwing away
his best chance by persisting in silence. Nothing in my opinion really can serve him
except opening his mouth."

"I admit the truth and reason of all you

say," she replied, "but faith is sometimes stronger than reason, and I have faith Scott is not guilty."

"Unfortunately a jury have to decide on facts, not faith," said Mr. D'Almarez rising to take his leave. "Of course, I shall do all in my power for him, and if he is found guilty, we must try to prevent his being hung; but I really think if he would only have placed full confidence in me, we might have got him off with only a sentence of manslaughter. Perhaps he may still think better of it."

" No," Grace answered, " I do not think he will—I hope he cannot. If after what he said to me to-day he were to confess that he did cause Mr. Brady's death, I should never be able to believe any one again."

" Ah! Miss Moffat, you do not know how great the temptation is to tell a falsehood if one is afraid of telling the truth. I do not quarrel with his statements on the ground of morality, but only on that of common sense; but then that is lawyer's way of looking at such things. It is not to be expected that a lady should take the same view. I trust it may all turn out better than I anticipate."

Miss Moffat drove back to Maryville in a very sad and perplexed state of mind; she had seen none of her friends at Kilcurragh, except that one at whose house her interview with Mr. D'Almarez took place, and she had no desire to see them. Amos Scott's position would, she knew, be the prominent topic of interest, and she did not possess sufficient moral courage to desire to combat popular opinion single-handed.

The more she thought about the matter the more conclusive seemed the lawyer's statements.

Notwithstanding her own determined advocacy, she felt that away from Amos her belief in his innocency was not strong enough to enable her to discard the extremely ugly doubts raised in her mind by Mr. D'Almarez's statement of the case.

Scott might believe that his sole chance of escape lay in reiteration of his innocence, and if this were so, Miss Moffat felt she could forgive his falsehood. What she could not forgive, however, was his religious hypocrisy supposing his statement untrue, and with feminine impetuosity she rushed to this conclusion—-

"If Amos be guilty he is the worst man in the world."

As there had been nothing in the conversation of a confidential nature, Grace repeated it to Mrs. Brady, merely omitting Scott's remarks about the dead man.

In silence Nettie listened to the end, then she asked,—

"Are you sure he said he could not remember where he left that stick?"

"Yes; he cannot even recollect where he went the day he lost it."

"That seems strange, does not it?"

"I think not, if you consider what he has gone through. He looks starved and ill, and bewildered. Oh! Nettie, the Scotts must have suffered terribly."

"I suppose so," said Mrs. Brady absently, as she sat looking out of the window with sad, weary, wistful eyes; and finding she showed no desire to continue the subject, her friend let it drop. Suddenly, however, Nettie rose, threw her clasped hands above her head, and, with a sigh which was almost a groan, hurriedly left the room.

Miss Moffat had become too much accustomed to these demonstrations of restlessness or grief, or whatever else the cause might be, to attach much importance to them, but still she thought it better to follow Nettie whom she found in her own room sobbing as if her heart would break.

Grace softly closed the door, and left her.

"Let her cry, poor thing," she thought. "It will do her good. After all, no matter what he may have been, he was her husband."

For the first time since her return to Ireland Grace that night slept soundly; slept a sleep unbroken by dreams; undisturbed by the perplexities that troubled her waking moments.

How long she had been in bed she could not tell, but at length from this depth of unconsciousness she was slowly aroused by little fingers that spread themselves over her face and hair, by a childish voice crying,—

"Oh! lady, please waken, please, please do."

Thus entreated, the "lady," for by this name Nettie's more especial favourite had elected to call Miss Moffat, struggled back to a due remembrance of where she was.

"What is it?" she asked between sleeping and waking.

"Mam-ma, oh! Mam-ma she frightens Minnie," explained the little one.

With an effort Grace roused herself fully.

"Minnie darling, is that you?" she asked, taking the child in her arms. "What has frightened you?"

"Mam-ma," repeated the shrill treble. "She talks so funnily—"

In an instant Grace had on her slippers and dressing-gown.

"I will go to your mam-ma, dear," she said; "but you must be very good and stay quietly here and go to sleep."

Then she laid the little creature's head on her own pillow, folded the sheet under her chin, gave her a parting kiss, and went into the next room closing the door behind her.

Dawn was just breaking, and without striking a light, Grace walked over to where Mrs. Brady lay, moaning and tossing, muttering words too indistinct to catch.

"Nettie," and her friend shook her vigorously; "Nettie,"—but no sign of recognition came. "Nettie dear, do speak to me,"—not a word of reply was uttered.

For a moment Miss Moffat stood helpless, then she went to that part of the house where she supposed Susan slept.

"I am so sorry to disturb you," she said, after awaking the woman, with that courtesy which was a part of her nature when addressing those below her in rank, "but I fear Mrs. Brady is very ill. Do you think you could go to the house of one of the men and send him for Dr. Girvan?"

"What is the matter with her?" asked the woman brusquely.

"I cannot tell; she is moaning and restless and does not seem to know me in the least."

"It's the fever, God help us," said Susan. "I'll waste no time, but go for the doctor myself."

"What! in the middle of the night?" exclaimed Grace.

"Ay, just as soon as if it was in the middle of the day," she answered, and proved as good as her word.

It was a long walk and a lonely to Kingslough, but Susan accomplished it, and brought back Doctor Girvan by the time the sun was rising.

Miss Moffat went down to speak to him, and asked Susan to stay with her mistress for a few minutes while she did so. Then the doctor said he would see the patient; and as Grace walked up and down the once neglected garden trifling away the time, he went into Mrs. Brady's room, the servant crossing him on the threshold.

He remained there a quarter of an hour or more, and when she met him Miss Moffat saw he looked ill at ease.

"Do you think there is anything serious the matter with her?" she asked anxiously.

"I cannot tell—yet," he replied. "You have been with her all night?" he said interrogatively.

"Yes, since I first knew she was ill."

"No one must go into the room but yourself and me."

"Why not?"

"You will know time enough. Amos Scott never murdered her husband at all."

"Then who did?"

"If you listen she will tell you."

And Doctor Girvan, looking grey and old and haggard in the morning light, drove away so utterly amazed and horror-stricken at Mrs. Brady's ravings that he forgot, if the fever were infectious, Miss Moffat stood a very fair chance of catching it herself.

CHAPTER XII.

TWO INTERVIEWS.

IT was a heavy oppressive afternoon—over Maryville a storm was brooding—the leaden sky seemed almost to touch the tops of the dark trees that hemmed in the house and grounds so closely that they might well have been likened to prison walls; not a sound within or without broke the stillness; in the fields the cattle lay panting with the heat; in the woods the birds kept silence, listening perhaps for the first roll of thunder, following swift after the leaping lightning.

It was a day to take the spirit out of any one, and Grace Moffat, as she sat alone in the large drawing-room, still insufficiently furnished, though some attempt had been made to fill its emptiness, felt miserable and depressed to a degree of utter wretchedness.

She had made up her mind what she ought to do, but she still hesitated and shivered at the idea of doing it. Nettie had been seriously ill for two days, and there could be no question that, although her malady had been at first merely inflammation of the brain, her disease was now complicated with the fever raging at the Castle Farm.

But Grace did not care for that—a new horror had cast out the old. If she had only been able to shake off the last task set for her, she would cheerfully have run the risk of contracting a dozen fevers; she had entreated Doctor Girvan to take it out of her hands, but he shook his head.

"Leave it till she gets better; there is time enough," he said, but Grace knew there was not time enough—that what she had to do ought to be done at once.

Sometimes she thought of writing to Lord

Ardmorne and requesting his advice and assistance in the matter; but having learnt all she knew through the delirious utterances of an unconscious woman, she felt herself charged with the weight of a fearful secret, which she was bound in love and honour to bear alone.

As for her tending Nettie without assistance, Dr. Girvan's medical sense had told him any such proceeding was impracticable, quite as soon as Grace's common sense had told her the same thing.

Without going through the ceremony of consulting him, Miss Moffat had despatched a messenger for her own little maid, mentioned once before in these pages.

"I want you to help me nurse Mrs. Brady, who is ill with FEVER," she wrote. "If you are afraid, do not come."

Back with the messenger, bundle in hand, came Nancy, trim and pretty as ever, radiant with delight at seeing her former mistress once more.

"What did your mother say, Nancy?" asked Grace, looking at the bright young face not without a certain feeling of remorse for having brought it to a house where death might be lurking for its owner.

"Say, Miss—nothing, to be sure; wasn't I coming to you!"

Miss Moffat walked to the window and back again, thinking in what form of words to tell the girl what she wanted with her.

"Nancy," she began, "if it had been only to nurse Mrs. Brady I required help, I would never have asked you to help me. Plenty of women older and more experienced than you could have been found for such a duty, but what I really require is a person whom I can trust to keep silence. I want you to promise me that to no human being now or hereafter—unless I give you leave—you will ever mention a word of what you may hear in Mrs. Brady's room."

"I'll be true to you, Miss Grace, what you bid me I will do; it's my right and my pleasure too."

Nancy had not been ten minutes installed in the sick room before Susan asked to speak a word with Miss Moffat.

"Now that you're getting your own servants here, Miss," she began, "you'll likely
not be wanting me any longer, and I just
want to say I'll go without any telling, if
you like."

"I am not getting my own servants here,"
said Miss Moffat, bewildered at the sudden turn
affairs had taken. "I do not want to meddle with
the arrangements of any other person's house;
but I cannot nurse Mrs. Brady alone, you
must know that, and I want to have some one
with me I can trust."

"You might have trusted me, Miss," said
the woman, with a smouldering fire in her dark
eyes. "The Lord knows you might. Even
though you have done this thing and brought
a stranger to this sorrowful house, man nor
woman shouldn't wring from me what I know,
nor—" she added after a pause, devoted possibly to conjuring up an effective finish to her
sentence, "wild horses shouldn't tear it. I
never did like the mistress, for all her pretty
face and quiet ways; but I came nearer liking
her the other morning than ever I did before,

when I found out how the trouble had been eating in like rust, when I heard her letting out everything she would have bitten her tongue off before she would have spoken in her right mind. It was her silence always beat me; but I'd have nursed her better than that slip of a thing can do, and I'd have died, Miss, before I let on she had been talking of anything beyond the common."

Miss Moffat stood silent for a moment, then she said,—

"I think open speaking is always a good thing. So far as I am concerned I should be quite willing to trust you. I have been so sure of your good faith, I never asked whether Mrs. Brady had been talking strangely after I left her and went down to Doctor Girvan, but—I do not want to hurt your feelings— how was it possible for me to let you nurse her? Do not imagine I am setting myself up as a judge of you or anybody else; all I ask is, if you had been in her place should you have liked such an arrangement yourself?"

The woman did not answer direct, but she broke forth,—

"Do you want me to leave?   I was fond of the children.   I did my best by them, I am doing all I know how now."

"No," Miss Moffat replied; "I do not want you to leave; at present, I may tell you, it would inconvenience me beyond expression if you were to do so.   When Mrs. Brady is better, no doubt she will wish you to go.   I say this frankly, but when that day comes, if you want a chance for the future, if you want to wipe out the past and try to make a better thing of the rest of your life, I will help you."

This time the answer came quick and sharp. "If there were more ladies like you, there would be fewer women like me," said the poor sinful creature; her assurance vanquished, her insolence gone,—and, throwing her apron over her head, she went along the stone passage leading to the kitchen, sobbing—sobbing every step of the way.

Which evidence of contrition touched Miss Moffat beyond expression, and gave her much hope concerning Susan's future.   She had learned many things during the previous twelve months, but she had still to be taught that repentance for past errors is not by any means a guarantee for future good behaviour; that the tears wept over a crime committed and irrevocable, dry up almost as soon as shed, and form no lake of bitterness across which humanity finds almost insuperable difficulty in steering to another sin.

Nevertheless, to be done with the subject, it may as well be here stated that Miss Moffat's generosity and Susan's impressibility between them bore good fruits.

The woman sinned no more. To the end of her life she was perhaps scarcely a desirable person to know, but she married respectably a man who was acquainted with her antecedents, and the pair migrated to a strange country, where their children and their children are working their way to name and fortune.

So goes the world—the busy, busy world we live in. How would the Puritan Fathers have looked upon the man who should marry a woman notable for antecedents such as these?

Still Grace sat looking out at the funereal
trees, at the garden full of flowers,—the common sweet-scented perennial flowers,—which
made many an otherwise poor home so rich
in colour and perfume before the present
bedding-out system was invented by ingenious
and enterprising nurserymen,—still she cast
an occasional glance at the threatening sky;
her thoughts divided the while between the
murdered man who lay in a quiet little burying ground amongst the hills,—his day ended
while it was still high noon, his power for evil
over, his ability to vex and distress gone,—
and the person who had dealt the blow which
silenced the beating of that wicked heart,
ended all its schemes, plots, hopes, purposes for
ever.

As yet she had not written to Mr. D'Almarez;
she had done nothing but think what had best
be attempted in the matter — what it was
possible to perform.

As to allowing things to remain as they
were till Nettie got better, she put that idea
aside as out of the question.   To Doctor

Girvan it appeared the only course to pursue; but then he shrank from responsibility. He was old, broken, feeble, and possessed of little moral courage; all his life long his *rôle* had been to know nothing, and pass from house to house leaving the secrets of each behind him, and why should he mix himself up with trouble and mischief now; or allow Miss Moffat to mix herself up in such an affair, if he could avoid doing so?

Grace, on the contrary, blamed herself for having permitted her own fears and disinclination to take so serious a responsibility on her own shoulders to influence her for such a length of time.

"If I can keep my own share in the transaction secret," she thought, "I should like to do so; but if not, and that unpleasant consequences ensue, I shall face them bravely as I am able. I wonder whether I could be punished. I wish I dare ask Mr. D'Almarez. Shall I write and put the question to Mr. Nicholson? No. I must wait no longer, whatever comes of it; no more time ought to be lost."

At this moment some one knocked gently on the panel of the drawing-room door, and thinking it could only be Susan or Mary, Miss Moffat said, " Come in," without turning her eyes from the window.

Next moment, however, some indescribable feeling impelled her to look round, and there standing in the open doorway, like a picture in a frame, was a tall bearded man who appeared as much astonished to see her as she was at sight of him.

" I beg your pardon," he said, " but I expected to find Mrs. Brady here. I asked for her and the servant pointed to this door."

" Mrs. Brady is dangerously ill," Grace replied; " with fever," she added, seeing the stranger advance into the room; then a second's doubt and hesitation, and she exclaimed, holding out her hand,—

" Why, it must be John Riley !"

" And you," he said, after an almost imperceptible pause, " must be Miss Moffat, though I should scarcely have known you."

" I have had little rest and much anxiety

since I returned to Ireland," she answered, as if apologizing for the change in her appearance.

He smiled gravely; it was not the right time, and he was not the right person, to tell her she had altered almost beyond his recognition, merely because she was now the most beautiful woman he had ever met.

"I thought you were in England," he said, putting aside the difficulty by changing the subject.

"So I was," she replied, "until very lately. I came over here directly I heard about Mr. Brady, and I am glad I did come, for Mrs. Brady is very lonely and very ill. And that reminds me you ought not to stay here."

"Why not?"

"For fear of infection."

"I have lived in a climate where fever is so common people forget to fear it," he said.

"But Mrs. Riley and your sisters have not," she suggested.

"I am not staying at Woodbrook," he answered. "I am at Lakemount, and the long ride back there will rid me of infection if I catch any here."

Not at Woodbrook! Time was when Grace would have asked him the why and the wherefore of such an extraordinary proceeding, but she could not do this now. Neither could he tell her what a grievous disappointment his return home had proved; how terrible that life of shortness, meanness, discontent, complaining, had seemed to him after the wider and nobler career his Indian experience had opened to him. He had done for his family all a man could, and his family were dissatisfied with his efforts. Not merely were affairs no better than when he went away, but they were infinitely worse. The amount of the mortgage was increased, the land was deteriorated in value, the houses and cottages were dilapidated, and in many cases almost falling to ruin, whilst Woodbrook itself gave evidence at every turn, of neglect; shortness of money; lack of spirit to improve; lack of will to make the best of a bad position; lack of faith that time and patience and energy might work wonders in the way of repairing even the shattered fortunes of the Riley family.

Naturally, when absent, a man forgets the failings of those belonging to him, if indeed he ever knew them; and perhaps there is no greater trial than for a person to return to the home of his youth to find it and the people it contains different from the ideal, experience of the world has been gradually working up for him.

But these were things of which John Riley could not speak to any one. Right glad had he been to accept Lord Ardmorne's invitation, and leave Woodbrook for Lakemount.

"Deserting his own flesh and blood," said Mrs. Riley.

"It does not seem to me that his own flesh and blood made things very pleasant for him," observed the General, his old spirit roused at the implied blame to his son.

Mr. John Riley's visit to Maryville was prolonged perforce; for he had not been seated many minutes before a flash of lightning, followed by a loud sullen peal of thunder, announced that the storm so long threatened had come.

During the time he remained he spoke of

little, except Nettie; her position and her
future prospects. He had been informed there
was no will, and that, consequently, the eldest
son taking the freehold property, Mrs. Brady's
share of her late husband's estate would probably be small.

"But, of course, all the children being
young, she will have an allowance for their
support," finished Mr. Riley.

"Money," thought Grace, " money again."

Had any one put the question, however, to
Miss Moffat, how people are in this world to
live without money, she might have been
slightly puzzled to tell them.

"If there is any way in which I can be of
assistance to Mrs. Brady, I should regard it
as a great kindness if you would let me
know," said Mr. Riley, when at length he rose
to go.

In her friend's name Grace thanked him,
and then he went on,—

"You have warned me against this fever,
Miss Moffat; but are you not running a
terrible risk yourself in the matter?"

"No," she answered; "I shall not take it."

"How can you be certain of that?" he asked.

"I have a perfect conviction on the subject," she said. "It is not intended I should have fever at present."

"Are you a fatalist?" inquired Mr. Riley.

"On some points, yes," she replied, and then he went; and Grace from an upper window watched him ride slowly away down the avenue, till the gloomy trees, dripping wet from the late storm, hid him from her sight.

For one second after she first recognized him, she had felt tempted to show her burden to this man who had once loved her, and ask him to take its weight and its responsibility. Only for one second. The formal Miss Moffat with which he addressed her cast the half-formed resolution to the winds.

How could she tell anything of the weary days, months, years, in which he had been schooling himself to forget the old familiar name, and think and speak of her only as Miss Moffat?

T 2

How could she, who had never loved him, understand the shock, the surprise, the misery, the pleasure, that sudden meeting had proved to him ! How was it possible for her to comprehend anything save that he was changed, that the John Riley of her childish and girlish recollection was gone as utterly as the years which were past !

Dimly and yet certainly, watching his figure as it slowly disappeared, Grace grasped the truth, that when she refused him that evening, while the scent of summer flowers was around them, and the sea rippled in on the shore, she killed the John she had known so long—been associated with so intimately.

That John was dead and buried ; and the John Riley, with the bronzed face and erect figure and bushy beard, who had answered her greeting so formally, was another man.

Over this interview, however, Grace had not much time to think. Another was impending that occupied her mind to the exclusion of almost every other topic.

" Shall I put it off ?" she thought; " the

lanes will be wet and the grass soaking."
And then she put the temptation from her.

"It must be done. Supposing I were to
catch this fever, who would there be to see
justice done; to save them both, if possible?"

If possible; she shivered at the suggestion
contained in the words.

She went to her room, in a different part of
the house from where Nettie lay; and putting
on her travelling-dress, an old bonnet and
coarse shawl she had found belonging to Mrs.
Brady, looked in the glass to see if in the dusk
might hope to pass through Kingslough un-
recognized.

"With a thick veil I think I shall be safe,"
she said; and then she took off the shawl,
carrying it over her arm, and put a thick lace
fall in her pocket, and taking the key of a
side-door with her, passed through one of the
drawing-room windows into the gardens, and
so made her way unobserved out of the grounds
of Maryville.

Once in the fields of the Castle Farm she
knew every inch of the country, and this

knowledge enabled her to reach, by unfrequented roads and by-paths, that part of the shore lying beneath the hill on which Ballylough Abbey stood.

There on a great piece of rock she sat down to rest, and wait till the twilight deepened and darkened.

When it was fairly dusk she resumed her walk, still along the beach, never entering Kingslough till she reached the further end of the town, whence through narrow lanes and back streets she arrived at Mr. Hanlon's surgery.

Her hand trembled so much at first that she could not pull the bell. At last she heard it tinkle, and to her great relief the door was opened by Mr. Hanlon in person.

" I wish to speak to you, if you please," she said, in a voice so low and quivering, that the poor attempt she made to disguise it was unnecessary.

" Certainly ; come in."

" In private," she suggested.

" You have come to tell me some great

secret, I suppose," he remarked jocularly; desiring, apparently, to put his timid patient at her ease. "Go in there," he added, pointing to a parlour beyond the surgery, where he had no doubt been reading, for a lamp stood on the table, and a book lay open near it. "Now what is it?" he went on, placing a chair for his visitor, and taking one himself.

She did not speak, but turned her head in the direction of the door of communication which he had left ajar.

"If you wish it, by all means," he said, answering that look, and he rose and not only shut but locked it.

"Now, what have you to tell me," he asked.

She put back her veil and looked him straight in the face.

As she did so, he shrank as though he had received a blow, and every particle of colour left him.

"Miss Moffat!" he exclaimed. "You in Ireland?"

"Yes; at Maryville," was her reply. "Now, you know why I am here."

" Wait a minute," he said, and unlocking
the door passed out into his surgery.   He was
not a man addicted to stimulants.   Even in
these days he would have been accounted ab-
stemious, and for those times when temperance
had scarcely established itself as a virtue, he
was reckoned, amongst wild young fellows
who knew no better, and old ones who ought
to have known better, a milksop who was
" afraid to take his liquor because he could not
carry it."

Now, however, he unlocked a cupboard, and
pouring himself out half a tumbler of raw
spirit, swallowed it at a gulp ; then he went
back and said,—

" No, Miss Moffat, I do not know why you
are here ; though I can guess why you might
have sent some one else."

" Who else might I have sent ?" she inquired.

" Why there is only one thing now to do, is
there ?" he retorted.

" What is that ?"

" Give me up as I have lacked courage to
give myself up," he said desperately.

"Then you do not deny it?" she said.

"Deny it! Why should I deny it? Have not I known it must come to this some time? Have I ever ceased cursing my own vacillation in not going straight away to the inspector here, and telling him the whole story? People might have believed me then; but they will never believe me now."

There was a moment's silence which he broke by asking,—

"How did you get to know about this, Miss Moffat?"

"Mrs. Brady is too ill to keep many secrets," was the reply.

"Ill! what is the matter with her?" he hurriedly inquired.

"Fever."

"Who is attending her?"

"Doctor Girvan."

"The old dotard will kill her," he exclaimed.

"He will do no such thing," answered Grace sharply. "Doctor Girvan will no more kill Mrs. Brady than you have killed Reuben

Scott. If she dies, it can only be because God willed she was to do so, not because she has lacked attention. Nevertheless," added Grace reflectively, " I should have had further advice, only I feared—"

" Do not let that consideration influence you any longer," he said, " I shall give myself up in the morning."

" Why do you say that?"

" Because there is nothing else to do," he answered with a bitter laugh. " Because the game is played out, and I may as well throw down the cards as have them taken out of my hands.

" Shall I tell you what you ought to do?" asked Miss Moffat.

" If you will be so good."

She took no notice of the mocking defiance of his tone, the recklessness of his manner with which he tried to cover the abject despair that was mastering him; but went on, gathering courage as she proceeded,—

" You ought to leave Kingslough at once. Scott can be saved without you; and Mrs.

Brady's name should be kept out of this miserable affair altogether."

" She is innocent," he said. " Tell me any form of words of I can employ, sufficiently strong to assure you of that, and I will use them."

Instinctively Grace drew back from the subject. " I am very certain she is innocent," she replied. " I require no assurance on that point from any one."

" I beg your pardon and hers," he answered; more humbly than he had yet spoken. " You are quite right, Miss Moffat," he continued, after a moment's pause. " If I stay here I may not be able to save my own life. If I go I shall spare her—perhaps."

" There is no perhaps in it. The greatest kindness you can do Mrs. Brady is to leave here at once."

" Leave, to be brought back," he said. " Fly, to make my return all the worse ?"

" There is no occasion for you to be brought back," she urged. " There is plenty of time for you to make your way to some country where you may be safe for the rest of your life."

" There is no time," he said; " once Scott's innocence is declared, the law will be on my track like a bloodhound."

" I have thought it all over," she persisted. "Scott's trial can, I am persuaded, be put off. Up to the present time, it may be supposed, no one knows anything of this except yourself and Mrs. Brady. Mrs. Brady is too ill to give evidence. Weeks must elapse before she can be questioned. Make use of those weeks. Go away as if for a visit, and stay away."

He put his elbows on the table and covered his face with his hands, and, as in some nightmare, the whole of his life passed in review before him. It had opened with such fair prospects; and behold, this was the end! He had hoped to win wealth, women's smiles, golden opinions from his fellows; and the end, was a choice of two alternatives:—to remain, and, if he escaped the gallows, be sentenced to transportation, most probably for life; or to escape, and lead a fugitive existence, under an assumed name, for the rest of his days.

He thought of the sacrifices his father had made for him; he thought of the castles his mother had built with her son's fame, or her son's talent, or her son's greatness for the foundation-stone of each; he thought of how proud he had felt of his own gifts; of how certain he had been of achieving success; and now he let his hands drop and looked at Miss Moffat with a face so white, so haggard, so aged, so hopeless, that Grace was forced to turn her eyes away. She could not bear to look upon a wreck so sudden and so complete.

"You ought not to be staying here," he said, in a choking voice and with an evident effort. "You came by the shore, I suppose? You would not mind, perhaps, if I asked leave to walk part of the way back with you. I mean, you would not feel—afraid."

"Afraid!" she only spoke that one word, but it was enough. He could feel there were tears and sorrow, and compassion and regret in her tone; tears, sorrow, compassion, and regret for him.

"If you will walk slowly along the beach I will follow you," he said. "I—I want to tell you how it all happened."

She bowed her head in acquiescence, drew the veil over her face once more, and passed out silently into the night.

She had not walked more than halfway to Ballylough Head before he was at her side.

Without waiting for him to speak, she said,—

"I do not know, Mr. Hanlon, whether you have a sister."

Under the circumstances it seemed to him a curious question, but he answered,—

"I have."

"Before you tell me anything, I want to know if I may, without giving you offence, speak to you as your sister if she were here might, and would?"

"If one of my sisters were speaking to me now," he replied, "she would not, I am very sure, find much to say that was pleasant. They have built their hopes on me, and now— but go on, Miss Moffat, say anything you like, no matter how true it may be, I will try to bear it."

"You mistake me a little, I think," she said; "all I meant was that if a sister found her brother in a sore strait as you are now, she would speak to him with no more reserve than I am about to do. Ever since I knew of this matter I have been thinking how it will be best for you to get away; what it will be best for you to do when you have got away. I suppose I am right in imagining you might find a difficulty in finding the means at once for a long journey."

"I have done very well at Kingslough," he replied, "and if I could only sell my practice, and I had an offer for it not long since, I should have no difficulty in going to the uttermost ends of the earth."

"Yes, but by the time you had sold your practice it might be too late. If you can get any friend to take your place while you go away apparently for a holiday, you had better leave everything just as it is at this moment. Woman's wit is quick, Mr. Hanlon, if it be not very profound, and my wit tells me every hour you lose in quitting Kingslough may prove nearer—nearer—that which we all want to avert. I have very little money here, but I can send you a letter which will enable you to get all you may require. You are not offended I hope?" she went on hurriedly ; "I know you cannot escape without sufficient money to do so, and it will be the happiest day of my life when I hear you have got safely out of the country."

All the manhood which was in him rebelled against having to accept such help as this; and for a moment he bared his head and let the cool night wind play upon his temples to relieve the pain which seemed tearing his brain to pieces. Never had Theophilus Hanlon seemed such a poor creature to himself before; no,—not even when he fled from the side of the man he had murdered; never had he been thoroughly humbled in his own estimation previously. If she had loved him ; if he could only for one moment have flattered himself she cared for him more than for the most ordinary acquaintance, the stab might not have pierced so deep.

As it was, he felt the wound was bleeding internally, and that it would continue to bleed at intervals throughout all the years to come.

"I have offended you," she said. "Pardon my want of tact. I did not mean to hurt your feelings."

"Hurt my feelings!" he repeated; in the interval during which he remained silent he had tested the truth of each word she said, and admitted, reluctantly it might be, but still certainly, that without such help as she offered, liberty and he might shake hands and part for ever. "Hurt my feelings! When a man has done what I have done, when he has failed to do what I have failed to do, he may reasonably be supposed to have no feelings left to hurt. And yet, Miss Moffat," he went on, "I will be frank with you; just for a moment your offer cut me. It is so hard—oh! my God," he broke out in a passion of agony, "what had I ever done that such a trouble should come upon me!"

"Hush!" said Grace. It seemed to her excited fancy as if in the darkness, his voice must travel more swiftly than in the light, to the Throne of Him whose justice and righteousness he questioned. "What have any of us done that trouble should not come? But in our eyes it does appear hard," she went on. " If you like—if it will not pain you—tell me how it all came about."

" I do not know how it began," he answered. "I supposed no one ever does. I could no more tell you how it was I came to care for Mrs. Brady than I could tell you how the grass grows, or the sea ebbs and flows. One thing, however, I do know, she never cared for me; never in that way. If she had, I should not be talking to you here now; if she had we would have been far away from Ireland long ago. I did not intend to tell her about it," he continued, " but one day it slipped out; and then she turned round and laughed in my face, such a mocking, despairing, forsaken sort of laugh, it rung in my ears for many a week after.

" ' Keep that for the next young girl you meet, Mr. Hanlon,' she said, ' who knows no better. I have heard it all before. Do you suppose I should ever have left my home, poor as it was, and my friends, few as they were, if he had not first thrown that glamour over me ? A woman cannot be deceived twice ; and there is no vow you or anybody else could swear, no temptation you could hold out, that could make me trust my future a second time in a man's hands.'

"She loved her children as I never knew a woman love them before, though she was afraid to show her affection, lest he should find means of punishing her through it ; and because I was kind to them, she had a feeling for me—gratitude, friendship, trust—I do not know what to call it—which would have prevented her from making any open breach between us, even if she had dared to tell her husband of the words I had spoken.

"But she did not dare to tell him. It was cowardly, I make no doubt, not to leave a woman so placed ; but except for me she was friendless, helpless, in the hands of a demon, and I could not keep from trying to know how things were with her.

"They grew worse and worse. After his attempt to get General Riley's estate failed,

the life he led his wife baffles description, and
yet she tried to hide what she suffered from
every one, even from me. She wanted him to
leave the country; she thought if she could
separate him from his bad associates, it might
be better for the children at any rate, if not
for her. I have seen her wringing her hands
about the stories which were told and the
ballads that were written and sung; and she
used to say she hoped it would be all gone
and past, all forgotten and put out of men's
minds before the children grew up.

"'For if not,' she asked, 'what is to become of them?'

"Then I prayed of her again to leave him.
I offered to get her and the children away
safely by some means if she would let me
arrange it all, and take them where he could
never find them.

"That time she did not laugh. She began to
tremble all over, and said,—

"'If you were a woman and made me the
same offer, I would go this hour; but if I did
what you want me, how could I ever look my

boys in the face when they grew to be men—
how should I teach my girls to be better than
their mother had been. I would rather kill
myself than do it. Never ask me such a thing
again.'

"I went out of the house ashamed, Miss
Moffat. I vowed to myself I never would ask
her again, and I kept as much away as I could
from Maryville, until after that morning when
she stole into Kingslough, and, half distracted,
tried to tear down the bills with which, as you
have no doubt heard, the town was placarded.
A man saw and pursued her. I happened to be
returning from a bad case which had detained
me all night, and she ran right up against me.
There was only one thing to do, and I did it.
I knocked the fellow down, and as she had
fainted carried her into my surgery. When
she was better I walked home with her, and
from that time began the mischief which has
ended as you know.

"So far as I could gather, the man I knocked
down bore malice, and took occasion, when he
was less than ordinarily sober, to jeer Mr.

Brady about there being an understanding between me and his wife. Mr. Brady forbade me to set foot inside Maryville, and I obeyed him until *that* night. Do I weary you ?"

"No," Grace answered. "I want to hear all you have to tell me. Some day she may be glad to have a person near her who knows the whole story."

"The evening before, Scott had been with me. He came in the worse for drink, and talked excitedly of the Glendares and Mr. Brady and his own wrongs. He said when Robert Somerford came to be earl, if he ever did, he would not have an acre to call his own ; that it had come home to the Glendares as it would come home to Mr. Brady ; and then he went on in a maundering sort of way to speak —forgive my mentioning the matter, but it is connected with that which followed—of what a blessing it was you had never after all taken up, as he styled it, with Mr. Somerford. ' Ay, it was a good and honest gentleman the first that asked her, if Miss Grace could have fancied him. There never was a Riley, Tories though they are, would have broken his promise, and brought a poor man to beggary, as Th' Airl has done by me.'

"'But,' he went on, 'Brady did not get Woodbrook from his wife's cousins, and it's like, clever as he thinks himself, he won't have the Castle Farm neither.'

"As the man spoke, it flashed through my mind that it was Mrs. Brady who had revealed her husband's designs on Woodbrook. I lay awake the whole night thinking about it, and then I understood dimly, but certainly, that when she wished to meet you, it was to tell you of his plans, when she wrote to you it was to entrust you to frustrate them."

"You are right," Grace remarked as he stopped for a moment, living, perhaps, the misery of that anxious night over again once more.

"What I suffered thinking about her and her position after that no one can conceive. I knew the man's nature. I had seen him mentally unclothed, and I was certain all she had endured previously at his hands would be nothing as compared with what would follow if once a suspicion of the truth entered his mind. I felt I must see her once again, and warn her of the danger that menaced. Whatever they might have been before, my feelings then were unselfish. You believe me, Miss Moffat?"

"I do, but pray go on."

"I knew he intended to go to Dublin the next day, and I saw him take the coach at Kilcurragh, where I made it my business to be. When I returned home, Scott had been round to say Reuben was worse, and so, putting some medicine for the lad in my pocket and Scott's stick, which he had left in my room the previous evening, in my hand, I started for the Castle Farm, taking Maryville on my way. I did not want any one at the latter place to know of my visit. Mr. Brady had put the last insult on his wife, and—"

"I know," Grace interrupted, "we need not talk of that—"

"After making sure there was no one about, I went into the flower-garden, and concealing myself behind some shrubs, looked into the room where she generally sat. You know it, the small apartment adjoining the drawing-room. She was there alone; and when I tapped at the window, seeing who it was she came and undid the fastening for me.

" 'I must speak to you,' I said. 'Will you come out, or is it safe for me to speak to you here?'

" 'Quite safe,' she answered, moving the candle so that no one from the outside could see me where I sat. 'Now, what is the mattter?'

" In a few words I told her what I suspected. She said I had guessed rightly.

" 'Are you not afraid,' I asked, 'of what may happen if Mr. Brady ever guesses it also?'

" 'No," she said; 'I do not intend to wait for that.'

" 'Do you mean that at last—' I began, scarcely able to believe the evidence of my senses, and in that very moment, when as it seemed all I had wished for was within my grasp, feeling a dull sick wish we had never met, that I had never loved, never tempted her.

"'No, Mr. Hanlon,' she answered; there was a composure and a peace about her I had never seen before; the hard restraint which usually characterized her was gone, and as she stood with the light streaming on her face, there was a hope which never previously shown in them gladdening her eyes. 'No, Mr. Hanlon, I do not mean that, and some day you will be thankful for it. What I mean is this, John Riley has come home. He is in Ireland; I could trust my life in his hands. He will protect me; he will enable me to get free from my husband, and to keep my children all to myself. If you still wish to serve me, you can see him and repeat what I say; you can tell him all—all you have seen in this house, all you know I have gone through, and bid him find some way of helping me as I found a way of helping him and his.'

"We talked for a little time longer, and then I left her. As I was going she noticed what a heavy stick I carried, and asked with a smile such as had never lighted up her face in my knowledge of it, whether I was afraid of being stopped that I walked about with such a shillelagh.

"I said it belonged to Amos Scott, who had left it at my place the previous night, and that I was going to take it to the Castle Farm.

"'They have fever there,' she remarked.

"'Yes, and a very bad fever too,' I said. "Every word we spoke that night is printed on my heart."

"'Poor people, how they have suffered!' she murmured, in a sort of whisper. 'Ah! they have felt what it is to be in his power as well as I."

"As I had come through the gardens, I returned by them. It was a quiet beautiful night, and not a sound, not even the flight of a night-bird broke the stillness.

"I went by the fields to Scott's house, and had got as far as the gate leading into the orchard, when I heard some one shout 'Halloa!' and a minute after a man came up panting to where I stood.

" It was Brady.

" I want to have five minutes' talk with you, sir,' he began, when he had recovered his breath a little, ' but not here. Walk on with me a bit down the road, where we shall be out of the way of eaves-dropping.'

" He had been so lately engaged in the same business that the word came naturally to him.

" To cut a long tale short, Miss Moffat, his journey to Dublin had been all a blind. He wanted," he said, " to know if the stories he was told of what went on in his absence were true, and he had returned to learn more than he bargained for.

" He went on for a time more like a madman than anything else; but at last calmed down a little, and said if I would promise him not to deliver Mrs. Brady's message he would over-look her ' Judasism '—so he styled her attempt to save her friends from ruin.

" This I flatly refused. I told him she had asked me to help her; and, heaven helping me, I would—"

The speaker stopped suddenly—he had been overwrought; he had been like a horse going across country till now; and now there came a double ditch, he remembered he ought not to have forgotten.

"Miss Moffat," he slowly recommenced, "after that came something I hesitate to tell you."

"Tell me," she said. "It does not matter that I am young instead of old. If it can help Nettie, it cannot hurt me."

"He bade me take her if she would. He said I had his full leave, and free to rid him of a wife who had been his curse from the day he brought her home—whom he hated—whom he might some day, and that soon, be tempted to kill."

"Yes!" gasped Grace.

"And I said I would rid her of him that hour and that minute; for that I loved, and honoured, and respected her too much to make her name a bye-word and a reproach, and that I would take her straight away from Maryville to her own kith and kin at Woodbrook, where there were two men who would know how to protect a woman's fair fame from a ruffian like himself."

" Yes ! " said Grace again breathlessly. The end was at hand.

" I turned to go back to Maryville. I swear to you, Miss Moffat, I should never have quitted the house, leaving her at his mercy, for I knew what she had to expect ; but he barred my passage."

" ' You villain,' he said, ' you shall never stir from here alive.'

" He put his hand in his pocket—I knew he went armed—and so I shortened the stick I held, turning it, and struck him over the head with the heavy end.

" I did not try to kill the man, God is my witness of the fact. In my examination I stated the simple truth. A man who meant to do mischief with such a blow could scarcely have dealt it. He dropped down on the instant, and then a horror seized me. I flung away the stick and knelt down beside him, and felt his pulse, and laid his cheek to mine.

"He was dead, and I had killed him. I heard footsteps coming and fled, thinking every moment some one was pursuing me. I have felt the same thing ever since. To-night you, Miss Moffat, have realized the ideal— that is, the end of the story I had to tell," he said in a low suppressed voice.

But Grace had something still to ask. "Mr. Hanlon," she began, "what did you mean to do about Amos Scott?"

"I meant to let him stand his trial, and if they found him guilty—confess."

"You are sure of that?"

"Yes, I think so."

"Then I think not, Mr. Hanlon," she said. "As the temptation mastered you so far, it would have mastered you further; and we may all feel very thankful that through Mrs. Brady's illness, you have been saved from so fearful an ordeal."

The words might be cruel, but the tone in which they were uttered took all bitterness out of them. It conveyed less a reproach for his cowardly selfishness than a feeling of gratitude that Scott's torture was well-nigh over, without it being necessary for Mr. Hanlon to criminate himself, or Nettie to denounce him. That she would have done so eventually, Grace could not doubt; but whether before or after the trial was another question. In any event it was well neither of them had been called upon to save Scott by such extreme measures.

By this time Miss Moffat and her companion had reached the plantations which divided the grounds of Maryville from the Castle Farm.

"Do not come any further," she said pausing. "I would rather you did not."

He attempted no remonstrance, but stood silent before her.

"By eight o'clock to-morrow morning," she said, "the letter I spoke of shall be in your hands."

He did not speak; he made no sign for a moment, then suddenly he broke out wildly,—

"I cannot go; it is useless. You ask more from me than I am able to do."

Utterly astounded ; utterly at a loss as to what he meant she remained mute, till suddenly comprehension came to her.

" Surely," she exclaimed, " you cannot be so mad as to imagine Mrs. Brady would ever voluntarily look upon your face again ! "

" Forgive me," he entreated humbly. " I was no more to blame for that outbreak than the patient who shrinks under the surgeon's knife. I know what I have to do, and I will do it. May God bless you for helping me upon my weary way."

He was turning to go without further leave-taking, when she held out her hand.

" Miss Moffat, you forget," he said.

" No, I do not forget," she answered. " Take it as a sign that the old has ended and the new begun."

Stooping down, he pressed his lips upon it ; then without uttering a word strode back along the path he had come.

She stood till she could distinguish his figure no longer, and watched him through the darkness drifting out of her life.

When she reached Maryville, she found Dr. Girvan waiting for her.

"I have come to tell you, Miss Moffat," he began, "that I am ashamed of myself, and whatever may come of it, good or harm, I will go to him, we both know about, and say just whatever you bid me."

"Thank you a thousand times over," she answered. "But I have been to him to-night, and he will leave Kingslough to-morrow."

"God be praised," exclaimed the doctor devoutly.

The opportunity was irresistible to Grace.

"I hope you are not premature in your thanksgiving," she said. "His successor may prove as great a thorn in your side as he has done."

"Ah! how can ye!" expostulated the old man, shaking his head reproachfully at her as he left the room.

CHAPTER XIII.

CONCLUSION.

IT was September—the loveliest month of all the year in Ireland. On the hill-sides the ripe corn stood gathered into golden sheaves. In the meadows—whence the small stacks had just been carried, to make the great ricks that caused many an humble farmyard to look full and wealthy—cattle browsed the rich pasture in a very ecstasy of content. Clear and distinct the summits of the distant mountains could be seen rising to meet the blue cloudless sky. Almost without a ripple, the Atlantic washed gently into sheltered bays, over sandy and pebbly shores. With as easy a

flight as that of the sea-birds, the white-sailed
vessels in the offing cleft their homeward or
outward way; whilst, on the hill-tops, the
purple heather and the yellow gorse mingled
their colours together, and wild thyme gave
forth its perfume in solitudes where there was
no passer-by to inhale its fragrance.

On the top of a slight eminence, from which
the ground, clad in a robe of emerald green,
sloped down to the water's edge, stood a
lonely-looking house, which commanded a view
—so its admirers said—of the Atlantic straight
away to Newfoundland,—two thousand miles
of ocean without a strip of earth; two thousand miles of water resting quiet and silent,
waiting for the stormy weather, when the
billows should rise up mountains high, lash-
ing themselves like a lion in his fury, and
rushing white crested to devour their prey.

This house had been taken by Mrs. Hartley
for the autumn, and to it, by slow stages, Mrs.
Brady and Grace Moffat were brought to
regain health and strength; the former with
pale face, and hair cut close like a boy's; the

latter weak as a child, after the mental excitement and bodily fatigue she had gone through.

By the time Mrs. Brady was pronounced out of danger, she had begun to droop; walking about Maryville—so Doctor Girvan said—like one more dead than alive, till Mrs. Hartley came and put a stop to her exertions.

It was marvellous to see the change that energetic lady wrought in the aspect of affairs. Before a fortnight was over she had discovered the house I have mentioned, which the gentleman who owned was glad to let, " in order to have the furniture taken care of," was his way of putting it; she had despatched Marrables, a cook, and her maid to have all in readiness for the arrival of the invalids; she had disposed of Nettie's children by sending them to a lady of limited income, who was " thankful," so she said, " to have it in her power to do anything to oblige dear Mrs. Hartley ;" and, finally, she had established herself and party at that precise part of the coast where Doctor Murney stated the air would be most bracing for Miss Moffat.

" Of course," said Mrs. Hartley to Nettie, "it does not matter to you where we go, provided we leave Maryville."

" No," Mrs. Brady answered; and that morning they drove down the gloomy avenue, and away from the gates of that house which had proved so wretched to her. She waved her hand back towards it with a gesture of farewell.

" Good-bye, Maryville," she said; " I may see you in my dreams, but never again with my waking eyes, I trust."

They had been but a few days in their new abode. Nettie, seated near one of the windows, was looking out over the sea; Mrs. Hartley was reading the 'Times;' Jet, apparently under the impression there was a fire in the grate, monopolized the hearthrug; and Grace was lying on a sofa, wondering when she should be strong enough to bathe, and walk, and climb to the top of one particular headland she could not lift her eyes without seeing.

" I think I should get well at once if I

could only lie for a few hours amongst the heather, watching the bees as they hum in and out amongst the thyme," she said at last.

"We will get some of the fishermen to carry you up to the top of the highest hill we can find, in a creel," suggested Mrs. Brady.

"I wish we could hear of a quiet pony she could ride," said Mrs. Hartley, in whose eyes the excursion proposed by Nettie did not find favour.

"I don't think a quiet pony was an animal Gracie ever much appreciated," retorted Mrs. Brady.

"I am very certain it will be a considerable time before she is strong enough to manage an unquiet one," answered Mrs. Hartley.

"You have never told me," said Miss Moffat, turning towards the last speaker, "how you heard I was ill."

"I heard you were ill," said Mrs. Hartley, taking off her eye-glasses and looking over the 'Times' at her questioner, "from John Riley. He said if I did not soon come over to Maryville I should hear shortly you were dead. I should have mentioned that fact before, but thought you were probably getting as much tired of hearing Mr. Riley's name mentioned as I was myself."

"I never intend to speak of John again," remarked Nettie. "I thought, Mrs. Hartley, you were his friend ; but I am sorry to find I was mistaken."

"My dear," said Mrs. Hartley calmly, "I hope I am Mr. Riley's friend, but still I can imagine many things more interesting and amusing than to hear his virtues recited every hour in the twenty-four."

"But you do not know all, or half ! Neither of you know how good he has been to me," exclaimed Nettie.

"If we do not we must be exceedingly dull of apprehension," replied Mrs. Hartley — at which Grace laughed, and remarked if they did not know, it was certainly not for want of being told.

"I never expected anything better from you," said Mrs. Brady, turning quickly towards her; "you never did appreciate John, and it seems as if you never would."

"Well, do not let us lose our tempers about him," entreated Mrs. Hartley, "more particularly as he is coming here next week."

"Is he coming?" asked Grace.

"Yes, to give us what I earnestly hope may prove the conclusion of the Scott romance. It seems to me that since I set foot in Ireland I have heard of nothing but the Scotts, the Glendares, the Rileys, the Hanlons, and the Bradys; interesting people all of them, no doubt, but I confess I like an occasional change of person and incident."

"So do I," said Grace. "Much as I like the Scotts, I shall be very glad when I hear they all are on their way to America."

"As if they could not have gone there as well at first as at last," observed Mrs. Hartley.

"I was willing for them to stay on at the Castle Farm, but Amos would not hear of it," explained Mrs. Brady.

"The moment, in fact, he saw he could go

the way he wished without opposition, all desire to do so ceased," remarked Mrs. Hartley.

"Still, I think it very natural he should wish to leave Ireland," said Grace.

"Yes, but would not it have been equally natural for him to wish the same thing eighteen months ago?"

"I cannot see it exactly," said Scott's apologist; and disdaining further argument, Mrs. Hartley resumed her perusal of the 'Times.'

From the foregoing conversation it will be inferred, and rightly, that influence had been at work in the Scott and Hanlon affair. The former was already at liberty, the latter beyond the reach of justice; at least, so far away that justice might be excused for not finding him. Nettie had made her statement, but this was so managed that those parts of the story which might have compromised her were kept in the background, and as no one wished to bring Mr. Hanlon to trial, it was extremely unlikely they would ever be elicited in Court.

To the wretched parents at Hanlon's-Town John Riley had broken the news himself. He had taken all care and trouble off Nettie, and she clung to him in her distress as a child might have done.

To him, nothing in Ireland seemed so unreal as the sight of Nettie in her widow's cap and black gown trimmed heavily with crape to express her mourning for the worst man and the worst husband, as Mr. Riley believed, who ever existed.

About Nettie herself, however, there was no pretence.

"I cannot say I am sorry," she confessed; "I cannot feel sorry. I wish I could, for oh! John, with all my heart and soul I loved him when I was a girl."

"Poor Nettie! poor little woman! I never repented but once making him marry you," he answered, stroking her thin face, "and that has been ever since."

"You did it for the best," she answered, "and in the worst of my trouble I never doubted that."

Why was it, Grace Moffat asked herself, that when she saw the cousins talking confi-

dentially together—saw John carry Nettie
in her first convalescence from room to
room, her head resting on his shoulder, her
arm thrown around his neck in her helpless
weakness—a pain went through her heart such
as had never struck it before?

"Am I jealous?" she thought, with an
uneasy laugh, "jealous of John! Absurd!
Am I jealous of seeing another woman prove
more attractive than myself? Yes, my dear
Grace, that is what is the matter. You are
growing old, and have got lean and ugly, and
you cannot bear that your friend should,
notwithstanding the troubles she has passed
through, keep her good looks whilst you are
losing yours. That is the secret of all this
dissatisfaction. Time was when you would
have laughed such an idea to scorn, in the
days   .

> " When I was young,
>   And had suitors, a full score."

Meanwhile Mrs. Hartley looked on, but said
nothing; not to Nettie, not to John, not to
Grace did she speak on the subject.

Only to Lord Ardmorne did she open her mind.

" I think if we have patience, my lord," she remarked uttering her oracle, " we shall see what we shall see."

At which his lordship smiled with a gravity befitting his station and his political opinions, and said, he " earnestly hoped so."

John Riley came as Mrs. Hartley said he would. He had seen the Scotts off. He went to Liverpool for the purpose. Amos was disturbed in his mind because at the last minute Mr. Moody had informed him there were no long-handled spades to be had in America, and he wished he had taken half-a-dozen out with him.

Mrs. Scott bade Mr. Riley say, if it cost twenty pounds, she would send the first cheese she made in the new country to Miss Grace. They had only one regret—that they could not take Reuben's grave with them.

" When I promised to put up a headstone and have the grass well kept," added Mr. Riley, " they began to cry ; but they were tears of happiness, so Mrs. Scott assured me."

Before Mr. Riley left, the quiet pony Mrs. Hartley had wished for was found; and Grace, taken by many devious paths to the top of a very high hill, where a throne was made for her amongst the purple heather, and the bees, as if to do her honour, never ceased humming in and out amongst the fragrant thyme.

But it was not there or then, with Nettie flitting round and about them, that John Riley spoke.

He waited till the leaves on the trees encircling Woodbrook had put on their October tints—till Grace was almost strong again—till it had been decided Nettie and her children were to go to England with Mrs. Hartley, and inhabit a cottage portly Mr. Marrables was despatched to inspect and of which he condescended to approve,—waited till the purple had faded from the heather and the Atlantic was beginning its winter wail of woe; then as they walked together by the sea, he said,—

"Lord Ardmorne has shown me how to save Woodbrook. It will require years — energy and hard work—but it may be done. When

Mr. Brady found he could not oust out my father, he wrote to Lord Ardmorne who would, he concluded, purchase the estate, offering to tell him, for a share in the profits, how its value might be doubled.

"To this his lordship wrote, declining all communication with him on any subject whatsoever.

"Since Mr. Brady's death, it has been ascertained what his scheme was, and Lord Ardmorne proposes I should take Woodbrook into my own hands, paying my father a certain sum sufficient to enable him, my mother, and the girls, to live comfortably, and myself carry out Mr. Brady's design. He has also offered me the agency of all his Irish estates, as Mr. Walshe has been given over by the doctors."

"And you will accept the agency and do as he so kindly suggests, of course?" said Grace, wondering why he paused so abruptly.

"It is not of course," he answered; "for the decision rests with you."

"With me," she repeated; "what can I have to do with the matter?"

"Everything," he said. "Grace, once before you refused me, and I went to India; if you refuse me again, I cannot stay in Ireland. With you I could accomplish what I have said—without you success would be worthless. If you say stay, I stay. If you say go, I go; and when once my father dies there will never be a Riley at Woodbrook again."

She hesitated and turned her head away, then with eyes still averted put out her hand timidly and shyly.

"Am I to stay?" he asked, taking it in both of his.

And she whispered "Yes."

"I have heard such a wonderful piece of news" said Mrs. Hartley, as John Riley and Grace entered the house together.

"What is it?" asked the former, thinking it could not be one-half so wonderful as the piece of news he had to tell; but with which, to do the lady's discrimination justice, Mrs. Hartley was already *au fait*.

"Cecil, Earl of Glendare is really married,

and Mr. Robert Somerford's chances of succeeding to the title are—*nil.* He is so disgusted at the turn affairs have taken that he has threatened to enlist if his mother and Mr. Dillwyn do not make some suitable provision for him."

"He ought to have gone to work and made a suitable provision for himself years ago," remarked Grace, running upstairs to take off her bonnet.

"She has promised to marry you?" said Mrs. Hartley.

"She has, indeed!"

It was quite true, and yet he felt scarcely able to realize to himself that the waves which once sung so sad a requiem to the hopes of his early manhood, had now murmured an accompaniment to the sweetest melody he ever heard proceed from human lips.

"Yes." That was the beginning and middle and end of the song; but it never ceased to gladden him through all the years that followed. And when John Riley forgets the sweet music he heard where the Atlantic washes that northern shore—the music which has made his life one long continuous har-mony—he will have forgotten every sound of earth.

THE END.

PRINTED BY TAYLOR AND CO.,
LITTLE QUEEN STREET, LINCOLN'S INN FIELDS.